DOC
SHADOWRIDGE GUARDIANS MC
BOOK 4

KATE OLIVER

This book is a work of fiction. Names, characters, organizations, places, events, and incidents are either a product of the author's imagination or are used fictitiously. Any resemblance to actual persons, living or dead, businesses, companies, events, or locales is entirely coincidental.

Written by: Kate Oliver

Copyright © 2024 Kate Oliver

"ALL RIGHTS RESERVED. This book contains material protected under International and Federal Copyright Laws and Treaties. Any unauthorized reprint or use of this material is prohibited. No part of this book may be reproduced or transmitted in any form or by any means, electronic or mechanical, including photocopying, recording, or by any information storage and retrieval system without express written permission from the author/publisher."

ABOUT SHADOWRIDGE GUARDIANS MC

Combining the sizzling talents of bestselling authors Pepper North, Kate Oliver, and Becca Jameson, the Shadowridge Guardians are guaranteed to give you a thrill and leave you dreaming of your own throbbing motorcycle joyride.

Are you daring enough to ride with a club of rough, growly, commanding men? The protective Daddies of the Shadowridge Guardians Motorcycle Club will stop at nothing to ensure the safety and protection of everything that belongs to them: their Littles, their club, and their town. Throw in some sassy, naughty, mischievous women who won't hesitate to serve their fair share of attitude even in the face of looming danger, and this brand new MC Romance series is ready to ignite!

Shadowridge Guardians MC
Steele
Kade
Atlas
Doc

Gabriel
Talon
Bear
Faust
Storm

ONE
HARPER

Mint chocolate chip.
Cherry Garcia.
Cookies and Cream.
Old-fashioned Vanilla.
Butter Pecan.

Her eyes scanned flavor after flavor as she tried to decide which one to pick. It shouldn't have been such a hard decision. Most people knew exactly what kind of ice cream they wanted when they walked into a shop. So why was it such a struggle for her to pick one?

"Next!"

Harper's eyes shot up to the person standing behind the counter, waiting for her to place her order. Her skin prickled with anxiety as she stepped forward and parted her lips to speak.

"What can I get for you, young lady?" the older man asked kindly.

She stared up at him for longer than was acceptable. Suddenly, she wished the floor would open up and swallow her whole. Instead of getting a cone, she should have gone to the store and bought a pint of something so she could've used self-checkout. It was the best way to avoid speaking to other people. But a pint of ice cream wasn't the same as having it in a sweet-smelling, crunchy waffle cone. Not even close. Besides, it had been ages since she'd treated herself. And thanks to her new job at the bakery, which was paying her more than she expected, she could afford a little something special.

Thankfully, the older man must have seen the panic on her face because he offered a toothy smile. "You look like you're having a hard time choosing a flavor. I'd recommend a scoop of the butter pecan along with a scoop of chocolate fudge."

Her eyes lit up, and she bobbed her head. It was like he'd read her mind. Or her tummy.

"And you look like a waffle cone kind of girl, am I right?" he asked.

"Y-yes."

Without further conversation, he scooped her cone. When he handed it to her, she thought her eyes might pop right out of her head. It was huge. Probably a pint per scoop. But her mouth watered in anticipation as she held up a five-dollar bill and waited for her change.

She turned to leave, then remembered her manners, so she whirled around and looked the man in the eye. "Thank you."

He winked at her, and she smiled in return before she made her way out to Main Street. There was a bite in the air, but the sun was shining. It was a beautiful day. Every day had been pretty perfect lately. *That's what happens when you're finally free to be yourself.* But today seemed better for some reason.

After she wove her way among people milling the sidewalks, she pressed the crosswalk button and waited for it to signal. She took her first lick and moaned. Butter pecan. So sweet and creamy. Definitely better than a store-bought pint. She couldn't remember ever tasting something so delicious. This treating herself thing might have to become a regular occurrence because, yum.

The signal changed, and she stepped off the curb. A roar of

motorcycle engines startled her. She was so focused on the delicious mix of butter pecan and chocolate that when one turned right in front of her, she yelped and jumped back. Two more raced by. She kept backing up, but when a fourth sped by, the rider revved the engine so loud it was deafening. She tried to run, but her feet tangled with one another. In slow motion, she went down. Her ice cream cone flew from her hand as she tumbled forward. Her knees landed painfully on the asphalt. Then her hands, which kept her from hitting her face on the ground.

"Ouchie!" she cried when sharp rocks dug into her skin.

Several more motorcycles raced past her, completely ignoring the fact that she'd fallen because of them.

"Move it next time," one of the men shouted.

Tears had already started falling. Harper was too stunned to move. Her ice cream cone lay several feet away, splattered on the ground. That made her cry more than the scrapes on her hands and knees. Well, until she saw she was bleeding. Blood always made things scarier. And being hurt always brought her Little side to the surface. She needed to keep it together, though. She was in public. The last thing she needed was to make more of a fool of herself than she already had.

"Shit!" a deep voice yelled.

A large man kneeled in front of her. His steel-blue eyes were wide with concern. She sniffled and brushed her tears away with the backs of her hands.

"Hey," he crooned. "You're okay. It's going to be okay."

His voice soothed her, but then she noticed his leather vest. A biker vest. He was one of *them*. She shrank back, scooting her bottom against the rough ground so she could get away. It didn't matter how concerned he looked or how handsome he was, she wanted nothing to do with him.

Panic tightened his features, and he held up his hands as though to show her he wasn't a danger. "I'm not one of them. I'm in the local motorcycle club here in Shadowridge. Those guys are from another town. I'm not going to hurt you. I'm a firefighter paramedic. Please let me help you."

A handful of people had stopped to watch the scene unfold, and suddenly, Harper was very aware of all the attention. She whimpered and lowered her gaze, using her long blond hair to shield her face from view. The man in front of her must have realized how uncomfortable it was making her because he looked up at the people standing around.

"Everything's fine here. Move along with your day," he barked at the crowd.

As though they took orders from him on a regular basis, everyone went about their business, leaving her alone with this stranger. This stranger who was looking at her like he actually saw *her*. And she wasn't sure if that was a good thing or not. Having such undivided attention was something she liked to avoid as much as possible. It was better to fade into the background. Staying invisible was the key to survival.

Cars zoomed past them. She needed to get out of the road and go home to lick her wounds. In private. Without the most handsome—yet slightly terrifying—man hanging around to watch. When she pressed her hands to the ground to push herself up, she yelped and plopped back down on her sore bottom. She brought her hands up and whimpered when she saw how scraped up they were.

"Ouchie!"

"Hey, let me help you. I have a first-aid kit," he said.

Before she could refuse, he scooped her up bridal style and carried her to a nearby bench where another man in an identical vest was standing. That man was much scarier looking. He was scowling, and when he pinned her with his dark eyes, she glanced away.

"She okay?" the man asked.

"She has some scrapes that need to be cleaned and bandaged, and then this Little girl needs a new ice cream cone."

Her eyes widened as she stared at the man who'd come to her rescue. Did he know she was Little? Was she that obvious? No. Definitely not. But she was sure he'd emphasized the word Little.

"Storm, can you grab my first-aid kit and a bear?"

A bear? Was she hearing things?

The second man grunted, then moved to where their motorcycles were parked. She looked at the first man, completely confused, but he just smiled and winked at her.

"I'm Levi by the way. My friend over there is Storm. What's your name, kitten?"

When her eyes widened at the pet name, he chuckled and pointed toward her backpack purse where she had a miniature stuffed kitten keychain hanging from the strap. Kittens were her favorite. They were so cute and fluffy. She definitely wasn't as cute as a kitten, but she kind of liked the pet name.

She pulled her bottom lip between her teeth as he looked over her knees. "Harper."

When he smiled at her, her heart pounded as though it was going to beat out of her chest. He was quite possibly the best-looking man she'd ever seen. Tall, dark hair, sparkling eyes, and a bright white smile. Not to mention the tattoos that were peeking out from the sleeves of his T-shirt.

"Harper's a beautiful name."

Heat spread to her cheeks, and she hoped they weren't bright red. "Th-thank you."

Storm didn't try to talk to her when he handed Levi a first-aid kit. She was glad for that. The man was…intimidating, to say the least.

"I'm going to clean up your owwies, okay? It might hurt a bit, but I'll be as careful as I can."

Not wanting to be a big baby in front of him, Harper shook her head. "I'll do it when I get home. I only live a few blocks from here."

Levi knelt in front of her and met her gaze. "It's better to clean them up now. Besides, you need another ice cream cone before you go home."

Yeah. It was quite sad to see her delicious treat splattered all over the street. What a waste. That alone made her want to start crying again.

"Hold out your hands for me, kitten."

When she obeyed, he flashed her a bright smile. "Good girl."

A shiver ran down her spine at his praise. The deepness of his voice did other things to her body too. Things that she wasn't going to acknowledge. Nope. Bad idea to go there. Men were on her hard-no list.

She watched as he cleaned her hands. Once he seemed satisfied, he applied antibiotic ointment and bandages, explaining what he was doing with each step.

"There. How's that?" he asked.

After she'd inspected her hands, she smiled and nodded. "Better. Thank you."

"Good. Now, while I do your knees, you can hang onto a friend," he said as he reached for the teddy bear Storm held out for him.

The bear was light brown with the softest fur she'd ever felt on a stuffie. As soon as it was tucked in her arms, she hugged it to her chest and sighed. Why did having a stuffed toy make everything seem not so scary?

"What kind of ice cream did you have?" he asked while he concentrated on his task.

"It was butter pecan and chocolate fudge," she answered wistfully. "It was so good. I can't believe I dropped it. The sign said I could walk."

His eyebrows furrowed. "Yeah, well, those guys are assholes. They've been riding through Shadowridge, revving their engines and running traffic signals for the last few months. It's starting to piss us off."

"Us?" she asked.

He glanced up at her briefly. "Yeah. My club. I'm a member of the Shadowridge Guardians MC. Have you heard of it?"

"No. But I'm kind of new here."

"Yeah. I thought so. I've never seen you before."

He applied the last bandage, then rose to his full height, which was pretty dang tall compared to her. At least a foot taller. Maybe more.

"Well, uh, thanks," she whispered as she stood.

Levi raised his eyebrows. "You're welcome. We're not done yet."

Huh?

"Let's get ice cream," he added.

She shrugged. "Oh, it's okay. I'm fine."

He gently nudged her back toward the ice cream shop. "Nah, Little one. After all that, you deserve a new ice cream cone. Besides, I think Storm would be sad if we didn't get him one."

The other man grunted and rubbed his stomach dramatically, though he was still sporting a scowl. "I'm definitely craving some cookies and cream."

She giggled. As scary as he looked, she hadn't expected him to be silly. It certainly didn't seem like ice cream was part of his daily diet. Both men were muscular and definitely worked out regularly.

When they got back to the shop, Levi opened the door and ushered her inside. It was empty this time, which she was relieved about.

The older man, who had helped her before, looked up from the counter and frowned. "Welcome back, young lady."

She smiled at him but didn't say anything as they approached the cash register.

"Hey, Tom. Harper had a little fall and lost her ice cream cone. Can we get her another one, please?" Levi asked.

Without missing a beat, Tom scooped up a new cone and

handed it to her. He shook his head when Levi tried to hand him some cash.

"No charge. What can I get for you and Storm?"

"Cookies and cream in a cup," Storm said.

"I'll take the same as Harper, but in a cup too. That looks pretty damn good," Levi replied.

Tom chuckled, then got the men their ice cream. They were totally missing out by not getting cones. Their loss.

"Thank you," she said softly.

Levi grinned and nodded. "You're welcome. Let's sit down."

When he pulled out a chair for her, she couldn't leave. She didn't want to, either. There was something about these two men that made her feel safe.

"So, what brought you to Shadowridge?" Levi asked.

She froze mid-lick at his question. She'd thought about how she would answer this question. In a small town like this, she knew people would ask. But the answer she'd practiced wasn't the answer she blurted out.

"I moved here to get away from my abusive ex."

TWO
DOC

Suddenly, the bowl of ice cream held zero appeal. All Doc could think about was finding the piece of shit who hurt the precious Little girl sitting in front of him. One look at Storm, and he could tell his friend felt the same way.

"Who's your ex? What's his name?" Doc demanded, more forcefully than he intended.

Harper's eyes widened. He needed to calm down before he scared her more than she already was. He'd seen the fear in her eyes the second he'd approached her. Now he knew the reason behind that fear. He wanted to hunt that fucker down and show him what happened when you hurt innocent women.

"I'm sorry, kitten. I don't mean to frighten you. I don't like abusers. If someone hurt you or is continuing to hurt you, I want to help."

He hoped his words would soothe her. From the way her eyebrows relaxed and her eyes sparkled at him, it worked.

"He's not hurting me anymore. I broke up with him a few months ago and moved here. He's pretty much left me alone since. I'm okay. I shouldn't have told you. It just sort of came out," she said, her gaze on her ice cream instead of him.

Storm sat back in his chair and crossed his arms. "If he's bothering you at all, you need to report him and get a restraining order. Or we'd be happy to pay him a visit."

Doc was glad his friend was speaking up too. He didn't want to come across as being overbearing or an asshole. Storm had no problem being an asshole, though. It was all part of his charm.

Her gaze skirted from Storm's to his. "He's not bothering me. I'm fine. I shouldn't have said anything."

He couldn't stop himself from reaching out to put a hand on hers. "I'm glad you did. We look out for the people here in Shadowridge. You chose a good town."

She smiled, then took a lick of her ice cream. Damn, Doc couldn't get the mental image of her tongue on him out of his mind. Fuck. Getting a hard-on was *not* something he needed right then.

"You said you live close by?" he asked.

"Yes. In the apartments off Grand."

That made him feel a bit better. There was only one complex on Grand. Though they weren't the nicest apartments, they were in a safe area. He'd still ask his brothers to start doing ride-bys from now on to keep an eye on things. They would do it without hesitation. Just as he would for any of them. That's why he loved his club so much. They all looked out for each other. And that included anyone who was important to them. He may have only known Harper for the last hour but there was no doubt in his mind she was already important to him.

"Do you work here in town?" Doc asked.

She nodded, her eyes sparkling. "Yes. I work at Dot's Bakery as the cake artist."

Doc grinned. He could picture her decorating cakes. Her long blond hair was partially pinned with barrettes that had miniature multicolored pom poms on them and her white fuzzy sweater with a big pink heart on the front screamed, "Little." The purple leggings and hot pink patent leather boots topped off the whole look. It was obvious Harper loved the whole rainbow of colors. Her cakes were probably beautiful.

He thought of Remi, his VP's Little girl, who was an artist. Remi was a goth girl at heart, but she secretly loved pink, and he had a feeling she'd go wild over Harper's boots. He could picture the two Little girls making art together.

You don't even know if she's Little and you just met her. Chill.

Storm smirked at him as though he knew what Doc was thinking, but instead of saying anything, he stood and tipped his head at Harper. "Nice meeting you, Harper. I'm going to go check on the bikes."

Doc nearly rolled his eyes at his friend. Could he have made his exit any more obvious?

"How's your ice cream?"

She took another lick and smiled. Doc shifted as nonchalantly as he could to relieve the ache between his legs. Fuck, it had been way too long since he'd been with a woman.

"It's good. Thank you."

"I'd like to see you again," he said.

Her eyes widened, and she froze but quickly recovered before she glanced down at her lap. "Uh, I...I don't...I don't mean to be rude. I'm not looking to date anyone. Not after..."

Shit. He should have thought of that. She had recently gotten out of an abusive relationship. Of course she didn't want to get involved with him.

Doc cleared his throat and nodded. "Right. Sure. I can understand that. Tell you what, I'm going to leave you my phone number, and if you change your mind or if you need anything, get hold of me, okay?"

He went up to the counter and grabbed a pen to jot down his number. When he handed it to her, their fingers touched, and he wondered if she'd felt the same jolt of electricity between them as he had.

"Would you like me to walk you home?" he asked.

"N-no. That's okay. Thank you for your help. And for getting me another ice cream."

"Take the bandages off tonight. Wash your scratches with warm water and soap, then apply some antibiotic ointment. Keep doing that twice a day until they scab over."

It didn't feel right walking out of the shop and away from her. He wanted to escort her home to make sure she got there safely. More than that, he wanted to spend every second with her that he could. He respected that she didn't want to date anyone. He would never cross her boundaries. But he still wanted to look out for her. Become her friend even. And maybe, eventually, she'd want more. He felt something for her. Something he hadn't felt in years. It was both thrilling and terrifying.

"It was nice meeting you, Levi."

He smiled and nodded. "Nice to meet you too, kitten. Remember you have my number. Call or text any time. Day or night."

It was painful to watch her walk away, but when she disappeared out of sight, he turned to find Storm staring at him with a smug look on his face.

"Dude, you were so obvious," Storm said.

Doc flipped him the bird. "Fuck off."

Storm laughed as they took off on their bikes down the street toward the Shadowridge Guardians MC compound.

Sweat dripped down his chest. His breath sawed in and out of his lungs. Memories of combat rushed through his mind as the fog of the nightmare started to clear. Doc scrubbed a hand over his face and squeezed his eyes shut.

When were the nightmares going to stop? It had been eight years since he'd served in Iraq. Surely, he should be better by now. At least, that's what he'd thought. Unfortunately, the experts told him otherwise. Even after all the therapy, it was possible to have PTSD for the rest of his life.

It had gotten better over the years. He no longer jumped at loud noises. He wasn't constantly distracted by visions of war. It was the damn nightmares that wouldn't go away no matter what kind of tea he drank before bed, or what exercise routine he tried, or what books he read. Some nights were worse than others. Tonight was one of those nights he knew he wouldn't be able to fall right back to sleep.

He tossed the blankets back and grabbed a shirt. Ever since a few of his brothers found their Littles, walking around the clubhouse shirtless was no longer an option. It was the quickest way for the men to get all growly and jealous over their women seeing other men half naked. He could kind of understand that. The thought of Harper seeing any other man besides him without clothes on made him want to punch something, and they weren't even dating.

A light was already on in the kitchen. That was the thing about living in the clubhouse. There were always people around to talk to when he needed it. He'd thought about getting his own place a few times, but being the club doctor, it was better for him to be close in the event of an emergency. Besides, between the MC and being on three-day shifts at the firehouse each week, there was no point in having his own place.

Gabriel, the club's chaplain, sat at the kitchen table with a mug in front of him, looking as tired as Doc felt.

He grabbed his own mug from the cupboard to pour some tea. "Hey, man."

"Hey. Nightmare?" Gabriel asked.

"Yeah."

This wasn't the first time the two men had met in the kitchen at midnight. They'd both served in the military, but while Doc still suffered from PTSD, Gabriel helped people with it. The chaplain had talked him through a bad night dozens of times. He was the only person in the MC who knew everything Doc had seen in combat.

"Want to talk about it?" Gabriel asked.

He shrugged. "Not really. It's one of the same ones I always have."

They sat together, drinking their tea in silence for several minutes.

"Why are you up?" Doc finally asked.

"I had a call." Gabriel worked as a counselor for a PTSD hotline. Sometimes the calls took a toll on him. He cared so much for people and their well-being. Doc knew his friend couldn't talk about the calls he took so instead of asking, he nodded.

"Heard you met a girl. Storm said she was sweet. Said she's the new cake artist at Dot's Bakery, and that you got her an ice cream cone," the chaplain said with a smirk.

Fucking Storm.

"Yeah. The Devil's Jesters were in town. Ran her right off the road in the crosswalk. She fell and scraped up her hands and knees. The poor girl was terrified."

"Storm said you took a liking to her."

Doc groaned. "Storm needs to get his ass kicked. I *helped* her. She was sweet and adorable, and I'm almost positive she's Little. She had these cute fucking barrettes in her hair with pom poms on them. And she had on a pair of hot pink combat boots. It was impossible not to like her. But she recently moved here to get away from her abusive ex. She's not looking for a new man."

Gabriel listened to him, and when he finished talking, his

friend smiled. "She might not be looking for a new man, but a good Daddy is a totally different thing."

He groaned and shook his head. "She said no when I asked to see her again. It's fine."

"Is she safe here from her ex?"

"She said she is. She lives in the apartments on Grand. I'm going to ask the guys to do some ride-bys to keep an eye on her place, though."

His friend chuckled. "Uh, huh. I bet you are."

After taking one last drink of his tea, Doc took his cup to the sink. "I'll see you in the morning."

Gabriel laughed as he walked out of the kitchen. Doc rolled his eyes, but a smile played at his lips at the thought of the Little girl with the kitten keychain and those damn barrettes. He hoped she'd change her mind and call him.

As he turned the corner to go down the hall, he bumped into Remi. She was Kade's Little girl, and her dad was a member of the MC. She was as much a part of this club as any of the men were.

"What are you doing up?" he asked.

She gave him a mischievous smile and shrugged. "I wanted to get a snack."

He tilted his head and studied her. Remi was a sweet Little girl but she was naughty. All of them were naughty. Ivy, Remi, and Carlee. And the three of them together were chaos waiting to happen.

"Night, Uncle Doc," she murmured as she turned in the opposite direction from the kitchen.

"I thought you were getting a snack."

She spun around and giggled. "Oh. Right. I forgot."

When she brushed past him, he sighed. Why did he have the feeling she was up to something?

THREE
HARPER

She sighed and ran the back of her hand across her forehead. It had been the longest day in the history of long days. Apparently half of Shadowridge was having a birthday, a wedding, or a baby shower this weekend. Not only had she decorated six cakes, but she'd taken eight more orders to be picked up the next day. Sheesh.

Harper looked down at her apron. She was a mess. Only an hour to go before Dot's closed. Then she'd be able to go home and soak in the tub. With her vibrator. While she fantasized about a certain guy who hadn't left her mind all week.

Every time she'd heard the loud roar of a motorcycle engine over the past few days, she'd practically given herself whiplash trying to see if it was Levi riding down Main Street. A small part of her had hoped he would come into the bakery to see her again. It was ridiculous for her to want that. She'd been very blunt with him about not being interested, and he seemed to get the message. It showed a lot about his character that he'd respected her wishes.

Stupid wishes.

Why did she tell him she wasn't interested? The man was

gorgeous. Tall and masculine but gentle and kind. Plus, she'd felt incredibly safe with him.

The sound of the bakery doorbell snapped her out of her thoughts. A few seconds later, the front counter clerk poked her head into the kitchen.

"Harper, one of our regulars is here to place a cake order."

She nearly groaned. It wasn't that she didn't want the orders. Staying busy was a blessing right now. It kept her mind off things, and she loved her job. All her favorite hobbies involved art, so being able to decorate sugary, delicious cakes for a living was definitely something she didn't take for granted.

"Okay, coming," she said before she quickly washed her hands and brushed off as much dried icing from her apron as she could.

When she stepped through the swinging door that separated the front of the shop from the kitchen, she smiled shyly at the customer standing at the counter.

The woman was dressed from head to toe in black. The only makeup she wore was a thick line of black eyeliner on her upper eyelid. As much as Harper didn't want to admit it, she was intimidated. Then all of a sudden, the woman smiled, and her entire face lit up as she held out her hand to Harper.

"Hi. I'm Remi. You must be the new cake artist."

Harper nodded and reached out to shake Remi's hand. "Yes. I'm Harper."

Remi rocked back on her feet and smiled. "Nice to meet you. I love your barrettes."

She couldn't help but reach up and touch one of the pastel-colored hair clips. She wore them to keep the hair out of her eyes while she worked, but it was an added bonus that they were so adorable. It was a tiny thing that reminded her she could finally be who she wanted.

"Thank you. Were you, uh, did you have an order to place for a cake?" she asked.

Remi seemed as though she suddenly remembered why she was there. "Oh. Right. Yes. I need a cake. Can you decorate it for me? Any chance you can deliver it?"

Harper looked up from the pad of paper she'd grabbed to jot down the order. "Oh, uh..."

The bakery didn't usually offer deliveries, but Dot, the owner, had said sometimes they made exceptions for known customers, and her co-worker *had* said Remi was a regular.

"Sure. Yep. Yes, I can deliver it. When do you need it?"

"Saturday?" Remi asked. "Yeah, Saturday night. I'm having a book club get-together and want a cake for it."

She nodded. "Right. Okay. And how big of a cake?"

Remi shrugged. "Enough for thirty people or so?"

"Wow. That's a big book club," Harper said as she wrote down the number of people.

"Yeah," she replied with a nonchalant shrug.

They spent the next few minutes going over the details of the cake. When Harper had all the information she needed, Remi handed her some cash.

"Thank you so much. Hey, do you like to read? You could join us for our book club. We'll be starting a new book this weekend. We like to read smut, though, so if you don't like dirty books, it might not be your thing."

Harper felt her cheeks heat, and she struggled not to smile. Not only was she being invited to hang out with a bunch of women who loved to read, but they loved the same kind of books as she did.

"Oh, uh, well, sure. I could stick around. That sounds fun. Should I bring anything?"

Remi grinned so wide that Harper was worried the woman's face might split.

"Nope. Just bring yourself and the cake. I'll have everything else you need. I mean, everything we need. See you there!"

Okay, that was a bit odd. But the woman seemed so nice,

and Harper was pretty sure they were close in age. Maybe she'd found a new friend. Starting over wasn't easy, and it would be nice to have some friends she could talk to. Although, based on all the black clothes the woman was wearing, it was likely she wasn't a Little. And that was okay. She could have vanilla friendships too. The world was her oyster. Or whatever that saying was.

Harper glanced at her GPS again. She hadn't missed any turns, but for some reason, she was driving in an industrial area. There were definitely no bookstores around here.

When the monotone voice told her to turn, she turned, then came to an immediate stop. Her eyes widened as she read the sign. *Shadowridge Guardians Motorcycle Club*. The large metal gates leading into the compound were open, and there were a few men standing outside talking. One of them noticed her arrival. When he started making his way toward her car, Harper felt herself shrinking back in her seat. The man was older but still intimidating. He was heavily tattooed with salt and pepper hair and a strut that told her not very many people messed with him and lived to talk about it.

Even though she saw him approach, she still jolted when he knocked on the window. With a trembling hand, she pressed the button to lower it.

"You lost, Little one?" the man asked.

"I, uh, I think so. I was supposed to deliver a cake for a book club, but I don't think the woman gave me the right address."

The older man's eyes crinkled at the corners as he smiled. "Ah, you must be Harper. Remi told me you'd be coming. I'm her dad. Name's Rock. Drive straight back to the clubhouse, and you'll see the front entrance. The book club is in there."

Wait. What? The look on her face must have expressed exactly what she was thinking because Rock chuckled and tapped the top of her car.

"Don't worry, Harper. You're safe here. Hell, I think this is the safest place in the entire town," he said.

She wasn't so sure about that. When he took a step back from her car, she eased off the brake and drove forward until she came to a building behind the first one. A row of motorcycles were parked out front and between the two buildings were several picnic tables along with a grill. For a motorcycle club, the place was surprisingly well-maintained. Not that she knew what to expect.

After pulling the cake from her trunk, she slowly approached the door. As she was about to reach for it, it flew open, and Remi bounded outside. And she was dressed from head to toe in hot pink. What in the world was going on?

"Harper! You came! I'm so glad you're here. My friends are so excited to meet you. Come in, come in."

Remi ushered her inside before she could ask any questions, and as soon as the door closed behind them, the room went quiet.

At least a dozen men and a few women were in the enormous space that housed a long bar and several pool tables. There were couches and tables and bean bags arranged randomly, but somehow it all worked to make the room feel comfortable.

"Harper?"

She knew that voice. She'd heard it in her dreams every night for the past week. Levi.

He stepped forward, his brows pulled together in confusion. Then he looked to Remi, and suddenly Harper felt a surge of jealousy. Were Levi and Remi a couple? Shit. That wasn't good. Did Remi know he'd asked her out?

"Oh, you two know each other?" Remi asked him with feigned innocence.

Levi arched an eyebrow. Another man with shoulder-length hair stepped forward, then wrapped his hand protectively around the back of Remi's neck.

"Remi, what did you do, Little girl? Are you meddling?" the man asked.

Harper looked from the man to Remi to Levi with wide eyes. What the heck was happening? She shifted slightly, trying to keep the cake from slipping from her trembling fingers. Levi must have sensed her nerves because he moved quickly to take the box from her and set it on the bar.

Remi shrugged. "I didn't do anything. I met Harper and I thought she might enjoy Book Club, so I invited her."

Levi glared at her. "Book Club wasn't even a thing until yesterday."

Wait, what?

"Don't be silly. I've been talking to my friends about starting a book club for months. We've had it all planned. You just didn't know about it until yesterday," Remi said, waving her hands in the air dismissively.

The long-haired man studied Remi for a long moment before he turned his attention to Harper.

"I'm Kade. Welcome to the Shadowridge MC," he said, holding his hand out to her.

Harper hesitated but reached out and shook it. Remi slung her arm over her shoulder and led her away from the two men.

"Come on, Harper. Doc is being weird. Let me introduce you to my friends."

"Who's Doc?"

Remi giggled. "Oh. Sorry. Doc is Levi. He was a medic in the army, and he's a firefighter medic here in Shadowridge. We all call him Doc because he's the club medical person."

Oh. Huh. She looked over her shoulder for another glimpse

of Doc. When she did, she caught his gaze immediately because he was still staring at her with a befuddled expression.

"He's single, you know," Remi said.

"Huh?"

She rolled her eyes. "Doc. He's single. Pretty hot, isn't he?"

Heat spread over her chest, and she lowered her gaze, trying to avoid giving herself away. Hot was an understatement when it came to Levi.

"Ivy, Carlee, meet Harper. She's new in town. I invited her to join us for Book Club."

The two women waved and stood.

"Nice to meet you. I'm Carlee."

"I'm Ivy."

Harper waved back. The women were beautiful, but they had an innocence about them she immediately felt connected to. Ivy was in a frilly pastel dress with lace ankle socks and a pair of Mary Janes, while Carlee was in a panda-bear onesie. She instantly felt comfortable with these women.

"Nice to meet you."

Remi clapped her hands. "Should we get started? We can all go into the playroom. I chose the book for this round so I have paperback copies for each of us."

The other women nodded and turned toward an open room lined with bookshelves. There were also several toy boxes along with some overstuffed chairs. Her Little side was jumping up and down over how cool the space was, but her adult side smiled and sat in one of the chairs while trying to ignore the toy boxes.

She could see Levi from where she was sitting since the room was basically an alcove off the main room. He was still staring at her as though he were trying to figure out a puzzle. When he noticed her looking, his gaze softened, and he offered her a gentle smile. All of this was so out of her comfort zone. When she'd left the bakery this afternoon, she'd thought she was going to some generic book club at a store or library or something. The last place she thought she'd be was an MC clubhouse with a bunch of tatted-up bikers and three women who seemed excited to have her there. Life was weird sometimes.

"The book I chose this week is called *Haylee's Hero Daddy*," Remi said, holding up four books.

Harper's eyes widened, and she started coughing. Had she heard right?

Carlee smiled and patted her on the back. "You didn't know we were Littles, did you?"

She gaped at the woman.

"Doc said he was pretty sure you were Little. When I came into the bakery, I knew without a doubt. You are, aren't you?" Remi asked.

With a slow nod, Harper looked across the clubhouse at Levi, who was watching her intently.

"He's a Daddy, you know. A good one," Ivy said.

"One of the best there is," Carlee added. "Even if he does tell our Daddies to give us enemas when we're not feeling well."

Cheese and rice.

What alternative world had she fallen into, and when was she going to wake up from this dream?

FOUR
DOC

"Dude, what the fuck did your Little girl do?"

Kade barked out a laugh. "I have no idea. Did you tell her about Harper?"

Doc thought about it for a second. "No, but the brat must have been eavesdropping the other night when I was talking to Gabriel."

Steele, the club president, chuckled. "Sounds like something she would do."

No matter how hard he tried, he couldn't keep himself from watching Harper as she sat with the other women and talked. They were being quiet, so Doc couldn't hear what they were saying, but when Harper turned to look at him with her mouth hanging open, he had a feeling the girls had dropped some kind of information bomb on her.

He wanted to go to her, scoop her up in his arms, and take her to his suite so he could have her all to himself for the night. It wasn't about sex. There was something about her that called to him. A vulnerability he wanted to protect.

"She seems sweet. Scared of her own shadow, though," Bear murmured.

"Her ex was abusive. That's why she moved here," Doc

replied.

Steele studied the group of women as he ran his hand over his chin. "We'll protect her. Whatever you need, just let us know."

Doc placed a hand on his president's shoulder. "Thanks, man. I appreciate it."

When he'd first gotten out of the military, getting used to civilian life had been difficult. Steele had invited him to the MC, and ever since, Doc had found the family he'd never had. All the men had helped him readjust to regular life, and in return, he'd become the club medic. He'd never be able to repay these men for helping to give him his life back.

He glanced at Harper again and smiled softly. She seemed to be having fun with the other Littles. They all had books in their laps, but none of them were reading. It seemed like they were having too much fun chatting.

"Are you going to have a talk with Remi about eavesdropping and meddling?" Doc asked Kade.

Kade grinned. "Oh, yeah. She'll be a very sorry Little girl once I'm done with her."

Doc nodded. "Good. Maybe she needs an enema while you're having that discussion."

"You know, I think you're right about that. It's been a while since she's had her bottom cleaned out. Maybe I need to do it more regularly because she's always better behaved afterward," Kade said.

Atlas, the club treasurer cleared his throat. "I think all the girls could use an enema. Carlee could for sure."

Steele grunted. "Same for Ivy."

"I'll leave the supplies in your suites," Doc said.

Not only was he the club medic, but he helped the men keep their Littles healthy too. Sometimes it bit him in the ass since the girls didn't always like the treatments he recommended and got back at him with little pranks and such. It was a small price to pay.

Hours passed. The entire time, Doc couldn't pay attention to anything except the Little girl in the other room.

It was almost nine o'clock when the women emerged from their meeting. Harper eyed him nervously with her backpack slung over her shoulder. She was leaving, and he felt a sense of loss at that. Even though she hadn't spent the evening with him, he liked having her in close proximity where he could watch over her.

"Thanks for inviting me," she said quietly to Remi.

Remi threw her arms around Harper. "I'm so glad you came. We'll have Book Club again in two weeks, but you have our numbers now, so we'll chat in between…about the book."

Carlee and Ivy giggled and nodded before they hugged Harper too.

Without thinking, Doc stood. "I'll walk you out, kitten."

Harper's eyes widened at the pet name, and a rosy red shade spread on her cheeks. He immediately felt bad. The last thing he wanted to do was embarrass her.

"Okay," she murmured.

He led her outside and reached for her car door as soon as she unlocked it. "Did you have fun tonight?"

She turned toward him, her blue eyes sparkling. "I did. I like them. It was nice to have some girl time. It's been a long time since I've had that."

"Because of your ex?" he asked, hoping she didn't notice him clenching his jaw.

Doc hated abusive assholes. He never understood how a man could hurt a woman or child.

"Well, yes. But I didn't do anything about it."

He stepped forward so he was nearly boxing her in against her car. "Kitten, I don't want to hear you take the blame for anything that asshole did to you. You *did* do something about it. You got the fuck away from him, and I'm proud of you for that."

They stared at each other for a long moment, both of them

breathing heavily. He felt a pull to lean down and kiss her but forced himself to ignore it. As badly as he wanted her, he wouldn't frighten her by being too forward.

"Thank you," she finally said.

"You're welcome. I'll tell you that whenever you need to hear it."

She shivered, and he stepped back and motioned for her to get in the car. She did, and he automatically bent down to buckle her seatbelt. He was reaching over her when he realized what he was doing.

"Sorry," he mumbled as he handed over the seatbelt.

When he heard the buckle click into place, he stepped back, resting his arms on the top of the car. "Listen, I hope you know I didn't have any part in your coming here tonight. I think Remi overheard me talking to one of the guys about you."

"I know," she said quickly.

"But, for the record, I'm glad you came. I haven't stopped thinking about you since we met. I kept hoping you'd call me."

It was risky to tell her all of that. If she wasn't interested, he'd get over it. Eventually. The last thing he wanted to do was put any pressure on her.

"I've thought about you too," she said, so quietly he barely heard her.

He stood a little taller. "Yeah?"

She nodded. "Yeah. I just…I'm not ready to date. I feel like I finally get to be myself again, and I don't want that to change."

He lowered himself to a squat so they were eye to eye. "First of all, a good man would never want to change you. He would want you to be yourself. Second, it's okay if you're not ready to date. I respect that. How about if we try being friends?"

Her wide blue eyes searched his face for a long moment before she nodded. "Okay. Friends works."

It wasn't exactly what he wanted, but it was a start. He nodded and rose. "Friends then. You have my number. When you think you might want to hang out, the ball's in your court."

"Okay. Thank you for being so nice to me, Levi."

"You're welcome, kitten. Will you text me when you get home so I know you made it safely?"

She looked up at him with the first mischievous look he'd seen from her. "Do you ask all your friends to text you when they get home?"

A smile spread across his face, and he winked at her. "Of course."

She giggled, and his heart soared. That was a sound he wanted to hear a lot more of.

"Goodnight, Levi."

"Night, kitten. Don't forget to text me."

When she rolled her eyes and pulled her car door shut, he chuckled. She may have been abused before, but that Little girl still had plenty of spirit inside of her.

Remi and Kade were waiting for Doc when he went back into the clubhouse. Remi had a look on her face that told him Kade had already lectured her thoroughly. And though she looked regretful at the moment, Doc was under no illusions that she was sorry.

He raised his eyebrows at the Little girl. "So, what was that all about, Remi?"

She glanced at Kade, who also raised his brows.

Remi sniffed. "I heard you talking to Gabriel about her, and I heard you tell him you weren't going to try and date her because she wasn't interested, but I think she *is* interested."

He put his hands on his hips and gave her a stern look. "Whether she's interested or not is none of your business. She just got out of a bad relationship, and she doesn't want to start a new one. I wouldn't be a good Daddy if I tried to pressure her into something she's not ready for. Right?"

Remi's eyes flashed when she realized what he'd said. "Yeah, I guess you're right. I'm sorry, Doc. I think you'd be such a good Daddy, and I wanted to meet her for myself to get a feel for her. The second I saw her, I knew she was perfect for you. I still think she is."

His heart softened a little. Remi was naughty for meddling, but she wasn't wrong. There was something between him and Harper. Even if Harper wasn't ready for it yet. Was *he* ready? He'd avoided relationships for as long as he could remember.

Most women wouldn't want to wake up to a man having nightmares and then deal with the aftermath. It was the reason Doc hadn't had a sleepover with a woman since before he was in the army. Sex? Definitely. Sleepovers? Absolutely not.

"Remi, I appreciate what you were trying to do, but it wasn't the right way to do it. I'm glad you made friends with her. I think she needs some good, honest ones like you girls. And I hope you'll continue to be her friend after tonight. But no more getting in the middle of my business, got it?"

She nodded. "Yes, I promise I won't. But you won't give up on her, right?"

He thought about it for a moment. He definitely wouldn't give up on her. He would be her friend. He was pretty sure she didn't have any, so if that's all he could be for her, that was fine. He was Remi, Carlee, and Ivy's friend. He'd be Harper's too.

"I'm not going to give up on her, Remi. But I'm also not going to pursue her. I have to let her heal the way she needs to. I'll be there for her however she needs. But you have to respect that she needs her space and time to get over what she went through with her ex. I don't know the depth of it or how badly he hurt her."

Remi lowered her eyes. "I think he hurt her badly. She didn't go into detail, but from the comments she made, it sounded like he controlled everything, but not in a good way. I don't think she was allowed to have friends or make any of her own choices, and now she struggles with that. She couldn't decide what she wanted when I offered her several different drinks, and I saw her hesitating when she was trying to pick cheese from the charcuterie board."

With every word, his jaw tightened a little bit more. He didn't miss Kade clenching his fists too.

"I appreciate you telling me that. I hope someday Harper will feel comfortable enough to open up to me. Until then, I need you and the other girls to be there for her when she needs to talk to someone."

Remi nodded. "We will. We like her. She's so sweet. And funny. She's definitely a Little, by the way, in case you didn't already know."

Doc narrowed his eyes. "Are you getting in the middle of my business again, Little girl?"

Remi held up her hands, but the smirk on her face told him she didn't care one bit about the threat in his tone.

"I wouldn't do that. Definitely not. I was just letting it be known. We talked about it since the four of us are all reading a Daddy book for Book Club. Harper is definitely a Little. I think she's a small Little like me."

The thought of rocking Harper in his arms and holding on to her tightly, making sure she knew she was safe and secure, warmed him from the inside out. He wanted to be the security blanket she seemed to badly need.

"Well, I'm glad to know she's a Little. And that she's found some Little friends. But you'll let me know if her ex is bothering her at all. Yeah?"

Remi's eyebrows drew together. "Is he bothering her?"

"I don't know. She said he's not, but since he was abusive, there's a chance he could come after her for leaving him. So, if she mentions anything about him calling or texting or showing up at her place, you tell one of us right away. Do you understand?"

"Of course. I'll tell you right away."

Kade cleared his throat. "Remi and I are going to head to our suite. We're going to have a chat before bedtime. I also think my Little girl needs her bottom cleaned out before she goes to sleep."

Remi groaned, and Doc smiled as her cheeks turned bright pink.

He wrapped an arm around her and kissed the top of her head. "Goodnight, Little girl. Thank you for what you did. Just don't do it again."

"Okay," she mumbled. Kade nudged her toward their suite.

Doc knew, without a doubt, that would not be the last time Remi got into the middle of his business. But he wouldn't want it any other way. These little girls had become part of his family, and he loved them unconditionally. Even when they were naughty. Like he had told Harper, it was important they got to be themselves with the people surrounding them. He hoped one day he'd get the chance to show Harper that she could truly be herself around him because she was perfect just as she was.

His phone vibrated in his pocket. When he pulled it out and opened the text, he grinned.

Harper: *I'm home.*

Doc: *Good girl. Thank you for letting me know. Your doors are locked up?*

Harper: *Yes.*

Doc: *Good. I start a three-day shift tomorrow at the firehouse. You can text me any time, but if I'm on a scene, it might take some time to respond.*

Harper: *Um, okay?*

Doc: *Just letting you know in case you decide to text me again. Which I would really like, by the way.*

Harper: *Okay. I'll keep that in mind. Be careful at work.*

Doc: *Always. Night, kitten. Sweet dreams.*

Harper: *Night, Levi. You too.*

FIVE
HARPER

The number of times she'd read the text conversation with Levi was embarrassing. It was a quick and innocent exchange, but his simple praise warmed her from the inside out every time she read the words.

Since she was off work the day after Book Club, she spent it in her favorite onesie doing all of her favorite things. She colored, played with her favorite baby doll, read some of *Haylee's Hero Daddy*, and texted Remi, Carlee, and Ivy about it, then ate fun snacks while watching *Toy Story*.

Of course, she also checked her phone about a million times hoping she'd have a message from Levi.

He'd told her the ball was in her court and that he hoped she'd text him again. But making the decision to actually do it gave her anxiety. When she'd texted him to tell him she was home, it had been easier because he'd *told* her to do it. Making the choice on her own was impossible. If she did text him, she might come off as clingy or annoying, and if she didn't text him, he might decide he didn't like her. Not that it should matter since she wasn't ready for a relationship.

It was nearly dark out when her phone vibrated with a text

from a number she didn't recognize. Disappointment flooded her, knowing it wasn't Levi. When she opened the message, every muscle in her body tensed.

Unknown sender: *When are you going to stop being a stuck-up bitch and come home?*

Bitch was Zach's favorite pet name for her. It had been a month since he'd contacted her and three months since she finally found the courage to leave him. He should have gotten the point by now. She wasn't coming back. Not only had she moved to another town to get away from him, but she hadn't responded to any of the messages he'd sent. Obviously, he must have realized she'd blocked him since he was contacting her from a new number.

Her hands shook as she read the message over and over. Why wouldn't he leave her alone? She wanted to move on and forget he'd ever been part of her life. To forget about the narcissistic emotional abuse she'd endured for more than two years. The bruises he'd left on her arms from grabbing her and shaking her violently as he'd screamed in her face. The times she'd had to ice her cheek after being backhanded when she'd said the wrong thing or looked at him the wrong way.

The Little space she'd been in all day was gone in an instant, and all she wanted to do was crawl under the covers in bed and hide from the world. It was times like this she wished she had a sibling or best friend to cry to. Or that her mom was still alive. She didn't know Remi well enough to vent to her, so she'd have to deal with it by herself. Something she'd been doing for much too long.

After blocking his new number, she turned off her movie and went to her bedroom where she'd be surrounded by all her stuffed friends. She always felt better when she could snuggle with Whiskers, her favorite stuffie of all. Although the bear Levi had given her was quickly becoming a favorite too.

As badly as she felt like crying, no tears came. She'd cried enough over the years. Making her cry had been like a trophy for Zach. Like he was pleased with himself when he broke her down enough that she couldn't keep it together. When she'd left him, she'd vowed to never cry over that asshole again.

She stared at her phone. She wanted to text Levi. Even if he couldn't respond because he was working, she wanted to talk to him. He made her feel safe and seen. It was strange. She barely knew him, and he looked physically terrifying. His eyes were dark, almost black, but when he looked at her, they seemed to soften. She'd noticed it the first time they'd met and again when she'd gone to Book Club.

It took nearly an hour for her to work up the nerve to reach out to him. Then another fifteen minutes of typing a message and deleting it repeatedly before she was satisfied with it.

Harper: *Hi.*

The second she hit send, she smacked her hand over her forehead. Hi? Really? That was absolutely the most ridiculous thing she could have said. He was going to think she was weird. But almost instantly, her phone vibrated.

Levi: *Hi.*

Levi: *How was your day?*

She bit her lower lip, debating what to tell him. Up until an hour ago, her day had been great. Should she say something about Zach contacting her? No. Definitely not. They didn't know each other like that.

Harper: *It was good. I was off work. How was your day?*

Levi: *Good. Did some drills and responded to a couple of calls. What did you do today?*

Hmm. Should she tell him she spent the day in Little space? Remi, Carlee, and Ivy had made it clear that he was a Daddy. The idea of telling him felt too much, though, so she gave him a simplified version.

Harper: *I relaxed at home. Watched a movie and had snacks.*

There. That was light enough but still the truth.

Levi: *What movie did you watch?*

Crap.

Harper: *Toy Story.*

When the three dots didn't appear right away, she started to panic. He probably thought it was ridiculous that she spent her day off watching an animated movie.

A few minutes passed with nothing, so she put her phone down and sighed. Well, so much for that. Even though she was sad he wasn't interested after her answer, she was glad she'd told him the truth.

She'd repressed who she was around Zach because he thought it was some strange kink she was into. He wasn't open-minded enough to realize it was a way for her to cope with her childhood trauma. To deal with seeing her father get so drunk he couldn't remember the abusive words he would spew at her mother when he woke up the next day. Being Little was something she couldn't change about herself. It was who she was, and she was tired of feeling guilty for it. She would never hide that side of herself again.

An hour went by with still no response from Levi, and with every minute that passed, she felt more disappointed. It was stupid. She'd told him she wasn't ready for a relationship, and she'd meant it. At least she thought she had. The care and compassion he'd shown her the two times they'd met had been more than Zach had shown her during the entire time they'd been together.

The silence started getting to her, so she turned on another movie. *Finding Nemo* this time. One of her favorites. And she wasn't going to feel silly about it, either. If Levi didn't like her because of the movies she watched, it was his loss. Yep. She was not going to spend another minute thinking about him and his muscles and tattoos she definitely hadn't fantasized about running her tongue over.

She was halfway through the movie when her phone vibrated.

Levi: *I'm so sorry, kitten. We had a call. I should have told you that if we're in the middle of a conversation and I stop responding, it's because a call came in. When the alarm sounds, we drop everything and run.*

Levi: *Toy Story is an awesome movie. To infinity and beyond!*

As she read his second text, she giggled. He seriously knew a line from the movie? That was cute. What he'd said made sense, but after being ignored by Zach whenever she annoyed or made him mad, she was overly sensitive to not getting an immediate response mid-conversation.

Harper: *Oh. Okay. I hope everything went well on the call.*

A second later, her phone started ringing. Levi's name popped up on the screen and the corners of her mouth curved into a smile.

"Hello?"

"Hey, kitten," he said in a soft voice.

"Hi."

She could hear the smile in his voice when he spoke again.

"I'm calling because I want to make sure you aren't upset. I didn't mean to ghost you. I wish I would have thought to warn you ahead of time. I would never not reply unless there's an alarm I have to respond to."

His gentle and reassuring words gave her butterflies in her tummy. He didn't sound annoyed calling her to explain. Zach wouldn't have bothered. He would have been pissed if she'd questioned him.

"Okay. I understand."

"Were you worried, baby doll?"

How should she answer that? If she answered truthfully, he would know she liked him. They were only supposed to be friends. Right? As ridiculous as it sounded, it already felt like they were more than that.

"I, uh... It gave me anxiety. I thought maybe I said something wrong, or you thought I was stupid for watching a kids' movie."

She waited for him to laugh at her and tell her she was being overdramatic.

"Oh, baby. I'm so sorry I worried you. That was my fault."

Huh? He was taking the blame?

"I promise in the future I'll do my best to communicate with you better. The last thing I want is to worry you or make you feel anxious," he added.

Tears pricked her eyes. This man was so damn kind and sweet. She had no idea how to respond to that. She'd always been the one apologizing and begging for forgiveness.

"It's okay," she said through the tightness in her throat.

He let out a huff. "It's actually not. I don't know everything you've been through, but my mom had been abused before she met my dad. Years after, even though my dad treated her like a princess, she still struggled with anxiety and fear. I know it doesn't just go away. It takes time to heal and to know you're safe. You're safe with me, kitten."

The tightness got to the point where she could barely swallow. When she finally spoke, it came out strangled. "Why would you want to deal with me and my baggage if you know what it's like?"

There was silence for a long moment, and then her phone beeped, signaling an incoming video chat. From Levi. Her eyebrows pulled together as she tapped accept and watched his face appear on the screen.

"I want you to see my face when I tell you this so you know how serious I am," he said. "You are more than any baggage you might have. We all have things we deal with. I see you, Harper. I see every bit of you. The scared and anxious side, but also the soft, sweet, absolutely impossible not to adore side. I can go as slow as you need, but I'm going to show you how you deserve to be treated, baby doll."

A tear rolled down her cheek, and she quickly dashed it away. "You'll get tired of all of my insecurities and triggers," she whispered.

"Look at me, kitten. Good girl. Thank you," he praised. "I won't get tired of you. You're precious, and I'm pretty sure you're my Little girl."

She gasped at his admission. He couldn't possibly know that. They barely knew each other. She didn't know his last name. Or his family. Or his favorite food.

Did it matter, though? Did any of that small stuff matter? Because the small details didn't define the man. It was the big, everyday things that showed his real character.

"Who do you have there with you?" he asked.

Her cheeks flushed when she realized Whiskers was in the frame.

"Don't be shy, Little one. I want to get to know this side of you too."

His gentle encouragement gave her the push she needed to hold up her stuffed cat. "This is Whiskers."

"She's pretty. You like kittens, huh?"

"Yes. They're my favorite animal."

The corners of his eyes crinkled when he smiled. "I wouldn't have guessed."

She giggled. "They're so squishy and soft."

"Yeah. They are."

They stared at each other for a long moment, and when she yawned, he cleared his throat.

"It's getting late. You probably need to get to bed. What time do you normally go to sleep?" he asked.

"Uh, kind of whenever."

He nodded. "We'll have to get you on a bedtime schedule eventually. It's good for Little girls to have a regular schedule so they stay healthy."

She liked that he was talking about the future and wanting to keep her healthy.

"I'm on shift for another two days, but I was thinking maybe we could spend the day together this weekend? Maybe go to the zoo? They have big kitties there. It could be a special

Little day for you. We could invite Remi and Kade if it makes you more comfortable."

Her cheeks ached from how wide she was smiling. No one had ever invited her to do something so fun. And the fact that he'd offered to invite Remi and Kade to make her feel better meant a lot.

"I'd like that."

"Good. Me too. What's your bedtime routine? Want me to help? Do you read a story or anything?"

Gosh. If book boyfriends were a real thing, she was pretty sure Levi was one of them.

"Usually, I get ready for bed, and then read or watch a movie until I fall asleep."

He seemed to consider that, but he didn't say anything about it. Instead, he asked a question that made her blush more. "Do you use a pacifier or bottle at bedtime?"

She lowered her eyes from the screen, embarrassed to answer.

"Look at me, baby doll," he commanded softly.

When her eyes met his through the screen, she didn't see any judgment or sarcasm. He genuinely wanted to know.

"I suck on a pacifier," she answered quietly.

His eyes softened, and she could have sworn they got a little lighter as he smiled. "Good girl. Thank you for trusting me with that."

"Is that okay?"

Levi nodded. "Yes, baby. That is more than okay. Pacifiers are good for helping Little girls with sleep or anxiety or when they're not feeling well. I always want you to do what makes you the most happy and comfortable in that headspace. Make sense?"

Her mouth was hanging open. This man was from another planet. She was sure of it. But she didn't care. If he told her tomorrow he had to return to that planet, she would probably beg to go with him. She might not be ready for a relationship, but whatever it was that was happening between her and Levi, she didn't want it to stop.

SIX
DOC

Only two hours left before he could go home to the compound. He needed to try to get a full night of sleep before he took Harper out for a day of fun. They'd texted and talked on the phone almost non-stop over the past couple of days. In that time, the only time she'd opened up to him was when he'd asked direct questions. She was shy and unsure of herself. He was quickly learning she needed his prompting. Something he didn't mind. It gave him the control he liked so much.

It felt like they were really getting to know each other. He loved getting glimpses of her Little. She was precious, and she called to him in a way no woman ever had. She was his. He knew it. He had to move at her pace because she was still scared. He wanted to hunt down her ex and teach him a lesson. How someone could ever hurt that sweet woman was beyond him. The guy was a coward, that was for sure.

"Hey, man."

Doc looked up from the medical book he was reading and nodded. "Hey, King. What's up, man?"

King was not only a firefighter but also belonged to the MC, so the two men spent a lot of time together.

"Ready to knock off work and go have a beer. It's been a busy few days. Lots of calls."

There *had* been a lot of calls lately. It seemed like it went in waves. Sometimes were slower than others. Being so busy had been a good thing for Doc. Otherwise, he would have been texting or calling Harper way more than he already had been. He hoped he wasn't being too clingy, but he couldn't seem to help it. His mind was almost always on her, but when he was treating a patient, he was focused on doing everything he could to save them.

Before Doc could answer, the alarm went off. Another call.

"Fire on Grand Avenue and Sixth Street. Grand Avenue Commons apartments," the announcement over the loudspeaker said.

His entire body tensed. Those were Harper's apartments. Both men sprang into action, running for the fire truck and ambulance.

"That's where Harper lives," Doc yelled at King.

Even though King hadn't been at the clubhouse when Harper had come for the girls' book club, he'd heard all about her from the guys. Meddling assholes.

King nodded and jumped into the truck along with several other firefighters. Doc leaped into the driver's seat of the ambulance, and at the same time, his partner, Ethan, hopped into the passenger seat.

Doc held his phone out to Ethan. "I need you to find Harper in my contacts and try to call her. It's her apartment complex we're going to."

"No answer," Ethan announced a few seconds later.

"Fuck!"

Adrenaline pumped through his veins as he sped through town toward Grand Avenue. It was late and dark, and he couldn't imagine how scared Harper was. Was she hurt? Burned? His stomach rolled at the thought.

Every second that passed was torture. The firetruck pulled

into the parking lot first, with Doc right behind. Even though it was a complex, the apartments were set up as tiny duplexes, and from what he could tell, only one of the buildings was on fire.

"Go find her. I'll see if we have any injuries," Ethan said.

Doc jumped out and ran toward the scene. A group of people crowded together watching the fire. He searched for one face in particular, and when his gaze landed on it, he let out a whoosh of breath.

"Harper!" he yelled.

She was shivering. He rushed for her, and she flew into his arms.

"Shh. I'm here. You're safe, baby."

"It's my building on fire," she cried, her body going limp in his arms.

Fuck.

"Okay. You got out safe, and that's the most important thing. I'm so proud of you for getting out of there," he told her.

She was wearing only a nightie that fell to her knees and she didn't have shoes on.

Ethan jogged over to him. "No injuries. Why don't you put her in the back of the ambo so she can warm up."

Doc nodded and lifted her in his arms. She clung to him and buried her face in the crook of his neck. She smelled like smoke, and he wondered how long she'd breathed it in before she got out of there.

"Sit on the stretcher, baby. Here's a blanket."

He fussed over her for the next few minutes, covering her with several blankets, and then used a wet cloth to wipe the soot from her face. When she started coughing, he grabbed his stethoscope.

"How long did it take you to get out?" he asked as he pressed the device to her chest.

"I woke up coughing and then heard screams and someone

pounding on my front door. I didn't see any flames on my side, just a lot of smoke. I don't know how long it took me to wake up, though."

After listening to her lungs, he grabbed a bottle of water and held it to her lips. "Take some sips, kitten."

She reached up to hold the bottle, but he shook his head.

"Put your arms under the blankets. Let me take care of you," he said.

When she immediately obeyed, he tipped the bottle up so she could drink.

A few minutes later, King approached the back of the ambulance. "Fire's out. Looks like it started at her neighbor's place. Smoke damage is pretty bad on her side, but no structural damage from what we can see. She's not going to be able to go back in there for a week or so until the super gets a restoration company to come out and clean everything."

Doc nodded. He had no intention of letting her go back in there anyway. At least not for a few days.

"I have nowhere to go. I have to go back inside," she whimpered, her eyes wet.

"You can't, baby. There's too much smoke. Breathing it is unsafe. The entire building will have to be cleaned by professionals," Doc said softly.

When her bottom lip trembled, he felt like an asshole for having to tell her no.

"Tell me what you need out of there. Give me a list, and we'll get it for you," King said.

"I don't have anywhere to go," she said as tears started running down her cheeks.

Doc couldn't stop himself from reaching out to pull her to him. He wrapped his arms around her. "You'll come home with me and let me take care of you."

He felt her tense, but he wouldn't back down. She'd be safe with him. There were plenty of empty rooms at the clubhouse. She could have a space of her own. Although, he'd prefer it if she stayed with him where he could watch over her and take care of her.

"Tell King what you need," he said.

She sniffled. "I need clothes. A-and Whiskers. And my medicine."

When King looked confused, Doc said, "Whiskers is her stuffed kitty. It's probably on her bed."

King nodded. "Got it. I'll be back."

When they were alone, Doc set her on the stretcher again so he could see her face. "What medication are you on, kitten?"

Her cheeks turned pink, and he realized she was embarrassed. Nope. That wasn't going to fly. He didn't give a fuck what she was taking, but she needed to tell him so he could make sure it wasn't something that would cause problems for her with the added stress of the fire.

"I'm on an anxiety medicine," she whispered, her gaze averted from his.

Without hesitation, he reached out and cupped her chin so she had to look at him. "There is absolutely no shame in that, kitten. When I got out of the military, I was on anxiety medication for nearly two years."

Her eyes widened like she couldn't believe what he'd said. "You needed medicine? But, you're so…so strong."

He stroked her cheek. "Baby, just because you need a pill to help balance out the chemicals in your brain does not mean you're not strong. Our bodies do all sorts of different things and react to our surroundings. Plus, once you add genetics in there, more often than not, things don't balance."

"My doctor put me on them after I left Zach. I was so freaked out about leaving the house at first. I was afraid he'd pop up out of nowhere and hurt me," she said quietly.

She was still embarrassed, and he hated that for her. He would show her there was nothing to be ashamed of.

"That makes sense. When I got out of the military, loud noises got to me. If I heard one, I would get anxious and agitated. The medication helped, plus I went to therapy on top of that."

His own mental health was usually only something he talked to Gabriel about, but if it would help his girl understand there was absolutely nothing wrong with her, he would tell her everything.

"Thank you."

"For what?" he asked.

"For not making me feel like some kind of freak. Zach always said people who took medications were weak."

Doc let out a low growl. "Yeah, well, fuck Zach. That asshole can go kick rocks. He's a loser and an abuser."

Her eyes sparkled for the first time since he'd arrived on scene, and when she smiled at him, he felt his soul settle.

"Are you sure I can stay with you?"

"Positive. I live at the clubhouse. I have my own suite, though, so you'll have some privacy. The girls will be thrilled to have you there."

King returned with a bag of clothes and the stuffed cat Doc had seen during their video call. He also had a bottle of prescription medication that he handed to Doc.

"Thanks, man."

"No problem. I can run by the store after shift and grab anything else she needs so you can get her home and comfortable."

Doc nodded. Joining the MC had been one of the best decisions of his life. They were truly his brothers and had his back without question. Just as he did for them. They were a family, and they would accept Harper into their family too. He'd go as slow as she needed, but he knew one thing for sure.

She was his.

SEVEN
HARPER

She wasn't so sure about her decision to stay with Levi. Not that it had really been *her* decision. He'd pretty much told her. She didn't have any other options, so it was either stay with him or sleep on the streets because she'd rather be homeless than go back to Zach. Thanks to Levi, she wouldn't have to worry about that.

He stayed in the back of the ambulance with her on the way to the firehouse and even put her shoes on for her. She was quiet the entire time. She was exhausted, both physically and emotionally. The apartment manager had reassured her they would be contacting a restoration company first thing the next morning, but they didn't know how long it would take. Her anxiety was through the roof, and the last thing she wanted to do was embarrass herself in front of Levi…again. So she focused on counting her breaths in the hope she wouldn't have a panic attack.

When they got to the firehouse, Levi wrapped her in a blanket before they exited the ambulance and then held her hand as he led her inside.

"I need to fill out some paperwork, then grab my stuff. It won't take long. Why don't you curl up on the couch over there, and I'll be right out." He pointed toward a large common room.

No one else was in there, so she nodded. What she really wanted to do was follow him around like a puppy because she was feeling a bit more insecure and anxious than usual, but how weird would that be? He'd probably think she was needy and annoying.

He was only gone for ten minutes, and when he appeared in front of her, she was startled. She'd been dozing off.

"Can you walk, or do you want me to carry you?" he asked.

She sighed and pushed herself up. "I can walk."

They went outside, and she expected him to direct her to his vehicle, but a truck pulled up and stopped in front of them. Harper turned to look at him.

"I rode my bike here. You're too tired to ride tonight, so I asked Kade to come get us."

Her bottom lip trembled. He was going to have her ride with a man she didn't know. She'd met Kade once before, and he seemed like a nice enough guy, but she didn't trust him like she trusted Levi.

"Baby, what's wrong?"

"I can ride with you," she said, hoping he'd change his mind.

Levi's eyebrows furrowed. He reached out and cupped her chin. "It's not safe for you to ride. My bike will be fine here overnight. Someone can bring me to get it tomorrow."

Oh... *Ohhhhh*. He wasn't going to leave her. What an idiot. Of course, she would panic and think the worst.

He lifted her into the back of the truck and grabbed the seatbelt. Then he paused as though waiting to see if she would protest. When she didn't, he continued. His arm brushed against her sensitive nipple. Even though she was pretty much a walking zombie, her body still reacted.

Ten minutes later, they pulled into the MC compound. The

clubhouse was quiet. Levi led her through the common area she'd been in before and down a long hall with closed doors on each side. At the end, he pulled out a set of keys to unlock his room. She hadn't been sure what to expect, but it definitely wasn't the tidy, homey living room they first entered.

"This is nice," she said.

Levi smiled softly. "Thanks, baby. It works for me. Come on. I'll show you the bedroom and bathroom. You should probably take a shower to get all the smoke off you before you go to bed."

A shower sounded heavenly, but she wasn't sure if she could hold herself up for that long. He studied her for a long moment and must have thought the same thing.

"Maybe a bath would be better. Whichever you prefer," he added.

"A bath would be good."

He nodded. "You got it, kitten."

The bedroom was similar to the living room. Small, but tidy and comfortable. The bed was made, and the entire place smelled like him. She could get lost in that scent.

"I'll run you a bath."

Before she could protest and tell him she could do it herself, he disappeared into the ensuite bathroom. She followed him and sucked in a breath as her gaze roamed his form. He was kneeling in front of the tub, pouring bubble bath into the water. When he rose, she gulped and craned her head back to look up at him.

"Do you want my help, baby? I promise to be perfectly clinical. No funny business."

She giggled softly. "I can manage it."

He reached out and stroked her cheek. "Okay. I'll be right in the bedroom, so if you need help, just call."

When he left her alone, she stripped and submerged in the water that was at a perfect temperature. A moan slipped from her lips as she leaned back to soak.

The sound of knocking had her jolting up, causing water to slosh around her. Where was she? What was happening?

"Harper!"

Levi. Crap. She was in Levi's bathroom. Had she fallen asleep? Panic rose inside her as she looked around, unsure of what to do. Before she could get any words out, the door flew open, and Levi rushed in.

"Oh my God!" she screamed, using her hands to cover her breasts.

His eyes were wild, and his breath was coming in ragged pants as he looked down at her. "Fuck, Harper. Did you fall asleep? I thought something happened. I knocked three times."

He did? She hadn't heard that. He looked angry, and she immediately started to shrink down as small as she could. Would he scream at her? Call her names? Or worse?

"I-I—" she stuttered.

Almost immediately, his eyes softened, and he lowered himself to a squat. "Fuck, baby. I'm sorry. I didn't mean to frighten you. I was worried. I shouldn't have let you bathe alone after everything you went through tonight."

She still had her hands pressed over her breasts, and she was thankful for the bubbles blocking the view of the rest of her naked body.

"I dozed off. I'm sorry. I'm so tired," she said quietly.

He nodded and reached for the towel he'd put out on the counter. "I know, baby. Tell you what. I'm going to close my eyes and help you out of the tub."

She hesitated, but when he closed his eyes and held out the open towel, she pushed herself up and grabbed hold of his hand for balance. He wrapped the towel around her and didn't let go or open his eyes until she brought her arms down to keep it in place.

"Come on, Little one. Let's get you into bed."

There was a fresh nightgown that wasn't hers laid out on

the comforter. It was so pretty. Soft yellow with white daisies all over it.

"I borrowed one of Carlee's nightgowns from Atlas. King didn't grab any sleeping clothes for you. I'll get you some tomorrow. For now, will this work?"

"Of course. I could have worn one of your T-shirts even." Her cheeks immediately warmed at what she'd said.

He probably thinks you're an idiot. So needy.

Levi smirked and stepped closer to her. "You know, I think that's a great idea. I like the thought of you wearing my clothes. Marking you as mine to anyone who sees you."

Okay, well she hadn't expected that. Not at all. And why did being marked as his make her so squirmy? "Um, sorry, I didn't mean to…"

He flashed his teeth at her as he smiled. "It's okay, baby. You don't ever have to be sorry for saying your thoughts. Besides, now that you mentioned it, I can't stop thinking about it, so instead of the nightie, I'm giving you a T-shirt."

She averted her gaze and hoped her cheeks weren't bright red with her embarrassment. "It's really okay. This is cute, and so nice of Carlee to let me borrow it."

Her argument went unheard. A few seconds later, Levi was tugging a soft black T-shirt over her head. A shiver ran through her, and she bit her bottom lip to keep herself from smiling. She didn't know why she felt so hot over the idea of him marking her, but possessive Levi did things to her body that no other man had done before.

"King didn't grab any panties either. I think he knew I would have slit his throat if he dug through your panty drawer. Carlee sent a package of unopened underwear for you, though."

Harper choked on air as she processed his words. Was he being serious? Based on the smirk on his face, she figured he was totally kidding.

When he held up a pair of panties in front of her, her

cheeks heated. They were adorable and so Little. White cotton that would surely go up to her belly button with scalloped edges and tiny red hearts printed all over them.

Then, her cheeks went from warm to on fire when Levi knelt in front of her and held the underwear by her feet.

"Hold onto my shoulders for balance and step in."

Was he actually getting her dressed? Like she was too Little to do it herself? So many emotions swirled in her tummy. Embarrassment. Arousal. Shock.

She pressed her hands to his thick shoulders, shocked by how muscular they were. She'd known he was fit, but Levi was the type of fit that was lean. At least, until she put her hands on him. He might not have enormous muscles, but he was solid as a rock.

"Step," he said patiently.

He waited until she had both feet through the holes, then started tugging the material up her legs. When he reached the hem of the towel, he stopped.

"I'll give you some privacy and let you get them pulled up the rest of the way, then you can remove the towel. I'll be right back."

A pang of disappointment hit her. Had she been hoping he'd pull her panties up all the way? The way he'd been taking care of her was making her Little float right up to the surface. It was probably for the best he'd left her to finish the job. The last thing she wanted to do was go completely Little in front of him.

She had just dropped the towel in the hamper when Levi returned. He had something small in his hand, but she couldn't tell what it was.

"Do you need to go potty before you go to sleep?"

"No. I'm good."

He nodded. "Okay. Crawl into bed, kitten. I changed the sheets before I left for my shift at the firehouse, so they're clean."

They would be sharing a bed. Crap. She hadn't thought of that.

"I can sleep on the couch," she offered.

His brows pulled together, and his already dark eyes turned darker. "There is no way in hell you will sleep on the couch. I'm sleeping on the couch. You are sleeping in the bed where you belong. Now, get in."

The steel in his voice gave no room for argument, so she obeyed and got under the covers. When she was settled, he sat at the edge of the mattress next to her.

"Here. I don't know if it's the same kind of nipple you have on your pacifier, but we can get you a different one tomorrow if we need to."

He held out his open hand to show her a large pacifier. It was plain yellow, and it did have the same nipple as the ones she normally used.

She stared at it for a long moment, unsure if she should reach for it. She'd told him she used one at bedtime, but him knowing and him seeing were two different things. No one had ever seen her with her pacifier in her mouth. Zach hadn't known she had one. He would have made her feel like a freak if he had.

"Take it, baby doll. It will help you sleep. Besides, after all the stress you've been through tonight, I'm sure you need something to help soothe you."

The fact that Levi had been soothing her since the moment he'd arrived at her apartment complex was something she was going to keep to herself. Coming across as needy was the last thing she wanted.

"Harper, take it, baby. You don't need to be shy around me. I'm a Daddy. I know you're Little. I've taken care of lots of Littles over the years."

Her heart sank and her shoulders dropped. At least he was honest about dating a lot of Littles. It was a good reminder why she shouldn't get attached to him. He didn't want anything serious with her. Even he had said they could just be friends.

"Wait. Let's back up. I can see by your face that you think I meant something different," he said before he reached out and cupped her chin. "I'm the medic of the MC. Most of the men in the club are Daddies, so whenever their Littles aren't feeling well, the guys bring them to see me. Sometimes, I babysit for my club brothers, but I haven't had a Little of my own in a very long time. I thought I was doing fine being single. Until I met you."

Wow. Okay. Don't fall in love. Don't fall in love.

"I will always be honest with you, Little one. Sometimes when I'm doing exams or helping my brothers treat their Littles, I see them naked. I also give them enemas and take their temperature in their bottoms, but when it comes to them, I'm simply a medical professional. Nothing more."

She took a moment to process his words. None of this bothered her. But what about the enemas and taking temperatures? Would he try to do that to her? She wasn't sure how she felt about that. Part of her felt squirmy and her panties were damp, but another part of her wanted to run and hide with embarrassment.

Almost as if Levi could read her mind, he smiled. "You both love and hate the thought of that, don't you?"

No point in lying. She nodded. "Yes."

"Most Little girls feel that way. Don't worry, though. When you become my baby girl, you'll be so used to me taking your temperature and cleaning out your bottom that it will become part of your regular routine."

Her mouth dropped open into an *O*. Did he say *when* she became his? He chuckled deeply and stroked her cheek.

"Time for bed, kitten. It's late. Since you're off tomorrow, I want you to sleep in as late as you can."

She felt panicky as he stood. He was leaving her alone, and she wasn't so sure she wanted that. But she certainly couldn't ask him to stay with her. He needed to sleep too. He'd been on a three-day shift. Surely, he was exhausted.

"I'm going to take a shower, but I'll be as quiet as I can. Do you need a nightlight?

"Um, it's okay," she said.

He leaned over and captured her chin, then stroked her cheek with his thumb. "When Daddy asks you a question, I want an honest answer. I can't take care of you properly if you're not honest with me. Do you need a nightlight, kitten?"

She trembled against his touch. Her heart was pounding so hard that she was surprised it didn't jump right out of her chest. Even though his words were gentle, he'd just scolded her. It did things to her body, but she was more focused on the fact that he'd called himself Daddy.

"Kitten."

"Huh? Oh, uh, yes. I prefer to have a nightlight."

"Good girl. I'll leave the bathroom light on when I'm done. For now, I'll leave the bedroom door open so you get some light from the living room."

Her eyes felt heavy as she pulled the blankets up to her chest. Then she felt around for Whiskers, something she did every night when she went to sleep. When she remembered he was in a bag in the living room, needing to be washed, she sighed and hugged one of the spare pillows to her body. The pacifier he'd brought her was on the mattress next to her. She stared at it for several minutes. Between not having Whiskers and not having a pacifier in her mouth, she would never fall asleep. Finally, she slid her hand out from the covers and slipped the nipple between her lips.

EIGHT
DOC

She was already fast asleep by the time he left the bathroom. He paused in the doorway and watched her for several minutes, fighting the urge to go over to fix her blankets and kiss her forehead. They weren't there yet. Keyword: yet.

He was still on an adrenaline high from responding to the call to her apartment complex. He couldn't remember a time he'd been so scared. It would probably take a couple of days to figure out the cause of the fire in her neighbor's home. If it was due to something faulty in the building, he would make sure she never went back to that place again.

After leaving the bathroom door slightly ajar so she had some light in case she woke up in the middle of the night, he grabbed a spare pillow from the bed, careful not to disturb her. He noticed her hugging one of the pillows and realized she had probably wanted her stuffed kitten. With that in mind, he went to the living room and tossed his pillow on the couch before he grabbed the toy and headed toward the laundry room.

Gabriel, Steele, and Kade were all in the kitchen as he passed by.

"Hey, man. Is Harper doing okay?" Steele asked.

He ran a hand over his face and nodded. He was wiped out. The only thing he wanted to do was go back to his suite, crawl in bed next to Harper, and rest. That wasn't an option, though. Even if they *were* more than friends, he would still sleep separately to protect her from his frequent nightmares.

Yeah, because every woman wants to have to sleep alone for the rest of their lives. Nobody is going to put up with that.

"She's good. Sleeping now. I think the shock will wear off by morning, and she'll be panicking more tomorrow about all of this."

"The girls will be around the clubhouse to be there for her if she needs some support," Kade said.

"If you need anything, we're here for you, man. We all support each other here," Steele added.

Doc knew that already, but it was nice to hear. Being part of the MC brotherhood was one of the best things that had ever happened to him.

"Thanks, guys. I'm going to go throw her stuffie in the wash. If you guys are up for a while, will you put it in the dryer on low heat when it's done?"

"You got it," Gabriel said.

By the time Doc dropped down onto his couch, he was beat. He was also thanking himself for recently spending the extra money on a new couch. It was much more comfortable than his last one. Especially since it seemed he'd be spending nights on it for the foreseeable future.

He could use one of the empty apartments to sleep in. Some of them were already furnished, but he didn't want to be that far away from Harper. What if she had a bad dream? Or needed a drink in the middle of the night? He wanted to be there for anything she might need.

So the couch it was.

He jolted to sit up, sweat coating his skin as the nightmare faded.

Fuck. Another one. It took him several minutes before his breathing was under control, but he couldn't go back to sleep. It was pointless.

He swung his legs off the edge of the couch, the cold, hardwood floor grounding him. The weight of his nightmare clung to his thoughts, refusing to dissipate. Rubbing his temples, he let out a frustrated sigh. Why did they always haunt him?

His heart pounded when he heard small feet padding closer. His girl was awake and coming to him. Had he woken her up? He didn't think he made noise during his nightmares, but he was never sure. Her presence alone brought him a sense of calm amid the chaos.

"Are you okay, baby girl?" he asked roughly.

She approached with hesitation, and he couldn't stop himself from letting his eyes roam over her bare legs. His cock twitched at the sight of her in his shirt.

He caught himself staring, heat spreading through his body. His girl had a way of making him feel like he was losing control, even in the most vulnerable moments. But now was not the time for desire. She was here because her home had nearly burned down, and it was his duty to be there for her.

She stopped a few steps away from him, her eyes searching his face for reassurance. Her hair cascaded around her shoulders, framing her delicate features. He longed to reach out and tuck a loose strand behind her ear, but he resisted the urge.

"I'm...I'm having a hard time sleeping," she finally admitted, her voice barely above a whisper.

He nodded and patted the cushion next to him. "Come sit, kitten."

"What are you doing awake?" she asked quietly.

Her voice held a hint of concern he could hear through the darkness. He hesitated for a moment, debating whether to share the truth or to brush it off. But his girl deserved honesty, even if it meant exposing his vulnerabilities.

"I had a nightmare," he confessed, his voice laced with emotion. "The demons from my past decided to pay me an unwelcome visit tonight."

Her eyes widened, filled with empathy and understanding. She took a step closer, her presence radiating comfort. She settled down beside him on the couch, close enough for their shoulders to brush against each other.

"Tell me about it?" she asked.

He took a deep breath. "I was in Iraq for eight years while I served in the army. I saw so many bad things, and even after all this time, I still have nightmares about it."

The weight of his memories pressed against his chest, threatening to suffocate him. But he pushed through, determined to share his truth with her. Even if it scared her away.

"In this nightmare," he began, "I was back in the desert. The sand was scorching hot, and the air was thick with tension. I could hear the distant sounds of gunfire and explosions echoing all around me."

As he spoke, she leaned closer, her warmth feeling like a lifeline in the darkness. He continued, letting the words flow out.

"I was surrounded by chaos and death, and I tried to save as many as I could, but I couldn't save them all. I watched my brothers die all around me, and I couldn't do anything to stop it."

When he looked down at her, her eyes were filled with tears shining in the dim light. It mirrored the pain he felt inside. She reached out and took his hand, intertwining their fingers. The bold move on her part surprised and pleased him.

The touch of her skin against his sent a surge of comfort through him, grounding him in the present moment.

"But you did save so many lives," she whispered, her voice filled with conviction. "You're a hero. Don't forget that."

He sighed, his grip tightening on her hand. "I wouldn't define myself as a hero. I did everything I could, though, but it doesn't make the nightmares go away. It's like they're stuck inside me, haunting me."

She nodded, her thumb gently caressing the back of his hand. "I can't pretend to fully understand what you went through, but I'm here for you anytime you want to talk. Or we can always sit in silence. I'm good at silence."

He smiled. The weight of his past lifted slightly as he took in her words. "Thank you, baby doll. It means a lot to me. You should go back to sleep, though. You need rest."

A few moments passed before she finally spoke. "Would you... Do you think I could lie out here with you? I don't want to be alone."

He looked at her, his heart swelling with affection for this Little girl who was quickly turning his world upside down. He couldn't deny her request, not when he knew firsthand the comfort that came from simply being near someone. And after what she'd gone through, he would be with her as much as she needed.

"Of course," he replied softly, scooting over to make more room for her to lie on the couch. She settled in beside him, her head finding its place on his chest, and he wrapped his arm around her protectively. The warmth of her body against his was soothing in a way he'd never felt before after having a nightmare.

As they lay there together, her breathing gradually slowed and deepened, signaling she had drifted off into a peaceful sleep. He watched over her, his eyes tracing every curve of her delicate features. In that moment, he had an overwhelming surge of hope she would give him a chance.

He watched her for hours, memorizing every freckle, curve, and dimple on her sweet face. When he couldn't keep his eyes open any longer, he closed them and let himself drift off.

When he woke up, the room was filled with soft morning light, casting a warm glow over their entangled bodies. His girl stirred beside him, her eyes fluttering open to meet his gaze. A small smile tugged at the corners of her lips, and he couldn't help but be mesmerized by her. She was so damn perfect.

"Good morning," she whispered, her voice filled with a mixture of contentment and vulnerability.

"Morning, kitten," he replied, brushing a strand of hair behind her ear.

"Did I hog the whole couch?"

He chuckled. "You did, but I didn't mind. For such a little thing, you sure do stretch out. But having you next to me was the best night's sleep I've had in a long time."

She blushed, her cheeks turning a delicate shade of pink. "I'm glad I could help."

They stared at each other for several seconds, their faces only inches apart. Slowly, he lowered his mouth to hers and brushed a kiss to her lips. It was quick and gentle, but he couldn't resist. When he pulled back, she smiled softly as she ran her index finger over where he'd just kissed her. He wanted to do it again, but he needed to take things slow. She needed time to adjust to his affection.

"Are you hungry? I smell pancakes. Bear usually makes them for the Little girls every morning."

Her eyes widened. "Bear? That's an ominous name."

He grinned, amused at her reaction. "Well, Bear may have a gruff exterior, but he's actually a giant teddy bear. You'll see. Remi, Carlee, and Ivy have him wrapped around their fingers."

She nodded, seeming intrigued but nervous. He couldn't

help the sense of protectiveness that washed over him. He wanted to shield her from any discomfort or harm, to make sure she felt safe and secure by his side.

After she pulled on a pair of leggings, they made their way into the kitchen. The delicious scent of maple and butter grew stronger. Bear stood at the stove, flipping pancakes with practiced ease. He had tattoos that covered both arms and a full beard that gave him a rugged appearance. Harper grabbed Doc's hand as they approached. He gave her a gentle, reassuring squeeze.

"Hey there, buddy," Bear greeted him. "And who's this sweet Little girl you've brought home?"

"This is Harper. She's mine."

Harper's head snapped back in surprise, and Doc realized he'd claimed her in front of at least a dozen people. Shit.

NINE
HARPER

It felt as though all eyes were on her, and she had no idea what she was supposed to do. Levi looked down at her, a silent apology on his face.

Bear cleared his throat. "It's nice to meet you, Harper. Do you like animal-shaped pancakes? How about a bear?"

Ivy snorted from the table. "When I asked for a bear, you said no."

"That's because you put salt in my coffee yesterday, brat," Bear retorted. "Harper looks much too sweet to do such a thing. Right, Harper?"

She giggled and shrugged. "Maybe. Maybe not. May the odds be in your favor."

As soon as she said the words, her eyes nearly popped out of her head. She wasn't normally so outgoing or smart-mouthed. Fear swirled in her tummy. Was Bear going to yell at her? Would Levi be mad that she'd embarrassed him?

Levi laughed and brought her hand up to his mouth to kiss it. "That's my girl. I like you sassy."

Wait, what?

She looked up at him and relaxed when the only thing she saw in his eyes was pure amusement.

When she moved her gaze to Bear, he winked. "Bear pancakes it is, princess."

"What are you girls going to do today?" Kade asked as he snatched a piece of bacon from Remi's plate.

"Hey!" she whined, but Kade laughed and kissed the top of her head, immediately quieting her.

Harper blushed at the affectionate display, feeling a mix of envy and curiosity. She had never experienced such an open PDA before. Her heart ached with longing. Is that what it would be like to have Levi as her Daddy?

"We were actually thinking of exploring the forest behind the compound. Harper, you can come with us," Carlee answered, a mischievous glint in her eyes.

"Absolutely not," Atlas said.

"No," Kade snapped at the same time.

Carlee's shoulders dropped. "Well, that's rude. Fine. We could have a tea party under the big tree. It's gonna be super nice outside today."

Steele nodded. "That's a much better idea. I bet you could talk Gabriel into making you some sandwiches so you can have lunch out there as well."

Levi squeezed Harper's hand gently, his voice soothing as he spoke, "Sounds like a perfect plan, Carlee. Do you want to join them, kitten?"

Harper nodded eagerly. "Yes, please. Can I?"

She hadn't meant to ask him for permission. It had felt natural. Everything between them felt natural. Sleeping in his arms had been like a dream. She'd never felt so safe with someone.

It must have been hard for him to share his nightmares with her, but it eased some of the doubt she had that he trusted her with something so painful. It made her think that maybe she could trust him too.

"Of course, baby doll. As long as you don't leave the compound without letting me know. Okay?"

"Okay."

A collective cheer erupted around the table, and Carlee jumped up, clapping her hands together. "Yay! It's settled then."

"Okay, we need to talk rules first," Kade said.

Remi groaned. "Always with the rules, Daddy. So many rules. It's not like we're going skydiving."

"Remi," Kade warned. "If you want to be a sassy Little girl, you can sit this one out and spend the day with a hot bottom."

Harper quickly averted her gaze, heat rising to her cheeks. The conversation had taken a sudden turn into territory she wasn't quite prepared for, but it ignited an undeniable spark of curiosity within her.

It was intriguing to witness this dynamic in a room full of people, but just like everything else with Levi and his friends, it felt normal. She was intrigued. A hot bottom. What would that feel like?

She felt a mixture of embarrassment and arousal at the visions going through her mind. The idea of being punished by Levi and experiencing his firm hand on her bare bottom sent a wave of desire coursing through her body. She wanted to experience that. She'd be trusting someone to take care of her, and that was scary.

Levi squeezed her hand. When she looked up at him, there was a mix of amusement and desire in his eyes. He leaned closer, his voice dropping to a low, husky whisper that sent shivers down her spine. "Kitten," he murmured, his warm breath tickling her ear. "I'm pretty sure I want to know what's going through that beautiful mind of yours right now."

A flush of heat spread through her body. When her mouth dropped open into an O, Levi chuckled.

"We'll discuss it later in private. For now, listen to Kade's rules."

Kade started listing things they could and couldn't do. She tried to listen. She really did. No going off alone. No jumping from tree branches. Nothing dangerous. But she couldn't focus. Her mind was reeling.

She glanced over at Levi, their eyes locking for a brief moment, and she could tell from the slight twitch of his lips he knew exactly what she was thinking. It excited and terrified her all at once. The connection they shared was undeniable, and in that instant, Harper realized maybe she was ready to explore her desires with him.

As Kade finished laying out the rules, Remi's voice cut through the tension. "Okaaaay, we get it. No running off alone, no climbing trees taller than Bear, don't eat any weird-looking berries. Can we go now?"

"Little one, you're about two seconds away from regretting your attitude."

Remi sighed. "Sorry, Daddy. I'm just excited."

Kade wrapped his fist around Remi's ponytail and pulled her head back to kiss her. "I know, baby. But you also know we would be devastated if anything happened to any of you. That's why we have so many rules."

Harper's heart raced the entire time she watched the two of them. The affection, the guidance...it was all so intoxicating. She wanted to experience that.

Levi leaned in closer as the couple continued to kiss, his voice barely above a whisper. "Don't worry, kitten. We'll have our own special moments together soon enough."

She turned to look up at him and nodded. Heat pooled between her thighs, and she bit her lip in anticipation. It scared her how much she wanted it to happen. She wanted Levi. She wanted to call him Daddy and experience the kind of special connection that Remi, Carlee, and Ivy so obviously had with their Daddies.

"I can't believe how big the compound is," Harper said as they meandered toward an enormous oak tree behind the clubhouse.

The entire place was surrounded by land. So much that she couldn't see the concrete walls the girls said lined the compound. The way the grounds were manicured, and how clean it was, made it obvious the guys cared about it.

"I've been trying to talk my Daddy into building us a treehouse in the oak tree. He keeps saying no. One day, I'll convince him," Carlee said.

Harper looked ahead to the tree. It was so big that they could probably build five tree houses in it. The branches were perfect for climbing on too. She could hardly wait. Apparently, it was the girls' favorite spot.

Ivy swung a picnic basket as they walked. Gabriel had ended up making sandwiches and snacks for them along with a thermos of tea for their tea party. It surprised Harper how much the men were involved in the Littles' lives. Not only did they have loving and supportive Daddies, but they had all kinds of Uncles who didn't blink an eye at stepping in when needed. It felt like they were all one big family. She was starting to realize she wanted to experience a life like that.

Even though she was excited to hang out with the women, the farther they got away from the clubhouse, the more she missed Levi.

Clingy much?

"You look smitten," Ivy said with a smirk.

Harper sucked her bottom lip into her mouth and glanced at the petite woman. She held a stuffed bear under her free arm.

When Harper hummed and shrugged, Ivy laughed.

Remi skipped up to them. She was dressed in all black except for the big pink bow in her hair. Harper loved Remi's style. Even if she'd never be able to pull it off herself.

"You like Doc. We can tell. I think he's in love with you," Remi said.

Harper burst out laughing. "Hardly! We barely know each other."

Ivy shrugged. "Doesn't mean he doesn't love you. I fell in love with my Daddy fast. We clicked immediately. He found me in a dumpster—a story for another time—and when he saved me, he said he knew immediately I was his. He took me home right after."

As they continued walking down the path, Harper couldn't help but let Ivy's words linger in her mind. Was it possible for someone to fall in love so quickly? She doubted it. Love was a complex emotion, one that required time and trust to develop. Didn't it? She certainly couldn't deny the strong connection she'd felt with Levi from the moment they met.

Carlee spread out an enormous quilt near the base of the tree, dropped her backpack onto it, and then sat. Ivy plopped down beside her with her stuffed bear still clutched tightly under her arm. When Harper lowered herself to the blanket, she sighed and looked back at the clubhouse.

"I'm scared to get involved with Levi. I was mentally, emotionally, and physically abused by my ex. He messed me up, and I don't trust easily. I'm scared of everything. I can hardly make a decision on my own. I'm a total wreck. He would realize quickly that I'm too much for him to take on."

Carlee raised her eyebrows and shook her head. "I don't think you understand these men. Doc would be the most amazing Daddy for you. He would cut off his dick before he ever hurt a woman. All the things you listed, those are all things he would love about you. He would love to make the decisions. He would love to be your protector and make you feel safe. Those men want to be needed. They want the control."

Remi nodded. "It's true. Even though I sass Kade about all the rules, I secretly love it when he goes over them before we go play. It's his way of protecting us and having control when he can't be there."

Harper listened to Carlee and Remi, and let their words sink deep into her heart. She'd never considered how someone like Doc could be her protector, her safe haven.

Lost in her thoughts, Harper barely registered when Ivy tugged at her arm. "What do you think? How do *you* feel about him?" she asked, eyes wide with curiosity.

Harper took a deep breath and met their gazes. "I like him. More than I probably should at this point. Maybe...maybe I should give it a chance," she whispered, surprising herself as the words escaped her lips.

Carlee grinned brightly and clapped her hands together. "Yes! That's the spirit. *Operation get Harper and Doc together* is under way."

The three women giggled while Harper tried to figure out what was so funny. A second later, Carlee pulled a notebook from her backpack.

"We have this notebook. It's a secret. The Daddies don't know about it. We pass it back and forth and add random stuff. When Remi went to the bakery and met you, we decided you were Doc's Little, so we wrote it in the notebook. It's called *Operation Doc and Harper*."

This time, Harper giggled. She loved that these women had so easily accepted her into their group. It had been so long since she'd had friends. Until she'd gotten away from Zach, she'd never realized how much he'd isolated her. It was fun to be able to talk openly with them and not fear their reaction.

Carlee opened the notebook, revealing a collection of doodles, notes, and secret messages. It was like stumbling upon a hidden treasure.

"I love this. It's so cool," Harper said as she thumbed through it.

"We keep it in the playroom behind the books on the second shelf, so if you ever want to add to it, you can. Just don't show Doc or any of the other men. It's our secret. We have a list of silly nicknames for the guys and ideas for getting them back when they do something to piss us off."

She giggled and nodded, then made an X across her chest with her finger. "Cross my heart. I won't say anything. I love all the stickers. It's so fun."

They talked and laughed the entire afternoon. Every so often, one of the men would walk out back and watch them but never approached. Ivy said it was their way of checking on them without interrupting their girl time. Part of Harper had expected Levi to come to get her at some point because she was spending too much time with her friends, but when he came out back, he stayed near the clubhouse and waved at her from a distance before he retreated.

When she looked back at the group, they were staring at her with dreamy smiles.

"Oh, yeah. They *love* each other," Carlee said.

TEN
DOC

"She's a sweetheart," Talon said.

Doc leaned back and smiled. He'd been doing a lot of that the past week. It was hard not to when his mind was always on the Little girl capturing his heart.

She was scared. But she was also letting him in slowly. It didn't matter how long it took until she felt completely safe with him. He would be patient.

"Yeah. She is."

Gabriel slid a beer to each of the men. "She's been through hell. I can see it in her eyes. She's scared."

He nodded. "I know."

Talon popped the top off his beer and took a long gulp. "Someone hurt her?"

"She's been through hell with her ex. I don't know the details. Only that it was physical and emotional abuse," Doc said softly.

Gabriel nodded in agreement, his eyes reflecting the anger they all shared toward any man who hurt a woman.

"She's safe now. We'll take care of her," Talon said.

He looked at his friends and nodded. "I know. Thanks."

Boisterous laughter drew their attention to the front doors.

Doc's gaze instantly went to Harper. She gave him a shy smile that had his insides melting and his cock jumping to attention.

Talon nudged Doc with an elbow, breaking him out of his trance. "Doc, you all right there? You look like you're about to fall head over heels."

He chuckled. "Fuck off, bro."

Gabriel snorted. "Seems to me like she's got you wrapped around her little finger already."

"Just you two wait until you find your Little girls. You'll be putty in their hands, and I'll enjoy talking so much shit."

Both men barked out laughter, but Doc ignored them as he got to his feet and went to Harper.

He reached out and gently brushed his fingers against her cheek. "Hey there, baby doll. Did you have fun today?"

She blushed and nodded, her wide eyes sparkling with an innocence that aroused him even more.

Doc let his touch linger on her cheek before he dropped his hand to his side. He couldn't help but notice the way her body trembled slightly as if she were still unsure of herself.

"I'm glad," he said softly, his voice filled with sincerity. "You deserve all the happiness and fun in the world, kitten."

"Thank you," she whispered.

He noticed dark circles under her eyes, and the tip of her nose seemed pinker than usual. Had she not been warm enough outside? She was probably still exhausted after everything she'd been through the night before and waking up in the early hours of the morning.

Carlee, Remi, and Ivy had already disappeared in search of their own Daddies, so Doc took Harper's hand and led her down the hall toward his suite.

"Where are we going?" she asked hesitantly.

"I'm putting you down for a nap."

"A nap?"

He nudged her inside and shut the door behind them. "Yes,

baby doll. A nap. You're tired. What kind of Daddy would I be if I didn't make you rest?"

She turned and swept her eyes up to his. "You'd still be a good one."

His heart squeezed in his chest. He hoped she meant that.

"Thank you, kitten. But you're still taking a nap. You look pale. Are you feeling okay?"

When he reached out and pressed the back of his hand to her forehead, he could tell she was warmer than she should be.

"I'm fine. I am tired, though," she mumbled.

"You're warm. I'm going to get some supplies. Go potty. Wash your hands when you're done," he said as he pointed her toward the bathroom.

When he left her to do her business, he stepped out of his suite, stopped at the community closet they had stocked full of supplies for Littles, and found a brand new baby bottle. After that, he went into his exam room and grabbed a thermometer and some medicine to help with a fever. Even though he'd taken care of many sick or injured men and Littles, his heart still thudded heavily in his chest at the thought of his own Little girl being ill.

Harper was standing near the bed when he returned. She seemed as though she'd gotten paler in the few minutes he'd been gone.

"Kitten, can Daddy get you ready for your nap?"

She thought about it for a beat before she nodded. "'Kay."

He moved to her and cupped her chin. "While I'm getting you changed, I'm going to take your temperature."

"Okay," she said.

"Do you know how Little girls get their temperatures taken, Harper?"

Her eyes suddenly went wide, just as he'd expected. This was all new to her.

"Remi said you take their temperature in their bottoms," she whispered.

"That's right. It's the best way to get an accurate reading. Will you trust me to take your temperature, baby?"

He waited patiently for her to decide if she could trust him enough for that. When she let out a deep sigh and nodded, he kissed her forehead.

"Good girl. I'll never betray your trust, Harper. If at any time, you need me to stop, you can say red, and Daddy will stop. You won't be in trouble, and I won't be mad if you say that word. It's called a safeword, and it's something I take very seriously. Understand?"

"Yes," she whispered.

She trembled before him, but he went to work, tugging her shirt over her head, then dropped to his knees to remove her shoes and socks. After that, he pulled her leggings down, leaving her in a pair of cotton panties and a thin bra. When he rose and leaned in to remove it, she shuddered and rested her hands on his chest. He was so proud of her for letting him take care of her in such an intimate way. As he pulled the material away from her breasts, he tried not to focus on her budded nipples. He had to remind himself that his girl was tired and possibly sick.

"Okay, baby doll, I want you to bend over the edge of the bed and relax your chest against the mattress. I'm going to pull the back of your panties down and spread some lube on your bottom hole before I put the thermometer in."

"Is it going to hurt?"

He smiled softly and shook his head. "It won't hurt, baby. It's going to feel odd and foreign, but it won't hurt. I promise."

She pulled her bottom lip between her teeth, slowly turned toward the bed, then lowered herself down.

"Can I have Whiskers?" she asked in a small voice that twisted his heart.

"Of course. I put him in the living room after I washed him. I'll grab him. Stay right there."

He quickly grabbed the stuffed toy and brought it to her.

When he held it out, she wrapped it under her arm and buried her face in its fur.

"Good girl, Harper. You're being so good for Daddy."

She shivered. "Thank you."

When he sat down beside her and pulled her panties down, leaving them bunched at her thighs, he noticed a wet spot. Unable to resist the urge, he glanced at her bare pussy lips and inwardly groaned when he saw them glistening with her dew. His baby girl was turned on by all of this, even if she didn't realize it.

Ignoring her wet pussy, he popped open the lid of a jar of petroleum jelly and scooped out a healthy amount. When he spread her cheeks with one hand, she let out a small whimper but otherwise didn't protest.

"Good girl. I'm so proud of you. I'm going to slide the thermometer in nice and deep now. Take a deep breath in then let it out slowly."

He waited until she started to exhale before he pressed the thick device into her bottom. She wiggled slightly but didn't fight him.

"Is it done?" she asked.

"Not yet, baby. It's in your bottom, but it needs to stay in there for three minutes. You're doing great. I'm going to wash my hands, and I'll be right back."

She nodded and squeezed Whiskers tighter. He moved quickly so he could get back to her, and when he sat down beside her again, he leaned back on his elbow so he could look at her face.

"You doing okay, kitten?" he asked as he brushed some of her hair away from her face.

"Yes. It's strange," she whispered. "And embarrassing."

He chuckled. "There's nothing to be embarrassed about around me, Little one. I've taken care of lots of Littles. I've taken their temperature, given them enemas, changed their diapers, and helped them on the potty. I love being able to take care of Little girls, and being able to take care of you is quickly becoming my favorite thing in the whole world. You'll get used to it, and you won't be embarrassed."

"I'm not so sure about that," she mumbled.

"You'll see," he replied as he sat up, reached for the thermometer, and twisted it in her bottom.

"Is it done, Daddy?" she whined.

He froze. Did she realize she had called him Daddy? Should he praise her for it? Would making a big deal of it scare her? Now probably wasn't the best time to discuss it. He needed to care for his girl.

The timer on his phone went off. He slowly pulled the thermometer from her bottom, smiling when he heard her let out a deep sigh of relief. His smile quickly disappeared when he read her temperature.

"Shit, baby, you're running a fever."

She twisted back and looked at him. "I am?"

"Yes. It's one-oh-two. Let's get you into one of my shirts and into bed. Then Daddy will give you some medicine before you take a nap."

He set the thermometer on a towel and quickly moved to get her dressed in one of his T-shirts. The last thing he wanted was for her to get chilled. With each passing minute, she seemed to get more and more lethargic, and that worried him.

"Crawl under the covers, baby. I'm going to get you an electrolyte drink."

When she was under the covers, he went to his small kitchenette and filled the baby bottle. The medic side of him knew this wasn't anything to panic over. It was a fever. She could be coming down with a cold or the flu. It was also possible her body was reacting to the stress of the fire. Nothing that medication, rest, and fluids wouldn't fix. The Daddy in him wasn't quite as calm.

Her eyes were closed when he went back into the bedroom. As soon as he sat on the edge of the bed, they fluttered open.

"I'm going to give you some medicine. It's liquid and tastes like grapes. Then I'll give you some juice."

She watched as he pulled the right amount of acetaminophen into a syringe. When he held the tip to her lips, she opened for him.

"That's my good girl," he cooed as he slowly squirted the liquid into her mouth.

"That's yummy."

"Yeah. I've found that Little girls tend to take their medicine without fighting me if it tastes good."

He held the bottle up. "This is juice that has electrolytes in it. I want you to drink as much of it as you can before you fall asleep. Do you want Daddy to hold it for you or do you want to do it?"

She hesitated for a few seconds before she held out her hand. "I'll hold it."

"Use both hands, Little one."

With both hands wrapped around the bottle, she brought the nipple to her lips and then glanced at him. He nodded his approval and smiled when she started suckling on it.

"Good girl. I want you to close your eyes and sleep. I'll stay here until you drift off. Then I'm going to go check on the other Littles to see if they're feeling okay. I'll take a baby monitor with me, so if you wake up and I'm not in here, call out for me and I'll come. Don't get out of bed unless you need to go potty. Understood?"

"Yes," she mumbled around the nipple.

She closed her eyes, and he couldn't resist reaching out to stroke her face. He hated how warm she still was, but the medicine would kick in soon enough. It only took a few minutes before her breathing evened out, and she started snoring softly, her lips going lax around the bottle. He gently pulled it from her grasp and replaced it with a pacifier before he grabbed the baby monitor and left the room.

He hated to leave Harper, but she needed to rest, and he had the baby monitor camera facing her so he could check on her. Besides, he needed to make sure the other Littles weren't getting sick.

Kade and Remi were the first ones he found when he got to the large community room.

"Harper has a fever. I put her down for a nap. You want to bring Remi back to the medical room so I can take her temperature and make sure she's not coming down with something?"

Even though he'd directed the question to Kade, Remi groaned and shook her head. "No. I don't have a fever. I feel fine."

Doc and Kade raised an eyebrow at the same time.

"Pretty sure that's not your decision to make, princess. Let's go," Kade said, holding his hand out for her.

She dropped her shoulders and stuck her bottom lip out. "I don't wanna get my temperature taken. I'm not sick."

When she didn't budge, Kade picked her up and followed Doc toward his medical room.

"Princess, we can do it the easy way or you can have a red bottom while Doc takes your temp. Your choice, but either way, it's happening," Kade said firmly.

Doc closed the door behind them and watched as Kade set a pissed-off Remi on the exam table. As soon as he let her go, she crossed her arms over her chest and huffed.

"Remi," he warned.

"I don't want an exam. I'm fine," she snapped.

The entire scene was amusing. Remi was always the one to fight her exams the most, yet she was also the one who always got the most turned on from them. Doc loved that she fought so hard, but by the end, he knew she'd be panting and mewling over being so exposed and vulnerable.

"Little girl," Kade said softly.

"*Old man.*" She glared at him. "Why don't you get a thermometer in your butt and see how it feels?"

Doc ran his hand over his face, trying to hide his quiet laughter. She was on a roll today. There was no doubt in his mind she'd have a red bottom by the time he got to take her temperature.

"Okay, that's it." Kade grabbed her by the wrist. In one swift move, he had her spun around so she was facing the exam table before he pressed his hand between her shoulder blades to bend her over.

"Daddy!" she cried.

"No. You had the chance to do this the easy way. Now you're getting a spanking in front of Doc. Then when I'm done, you're going to get your temperature taken, and you're going to behave while he does it, or I'll have him give you an enema too."

When her only response was a whimper, Kade tucked his hand in the back of her leggings and yanked them down—along with her panties.

"I'm sorry, Daddy. I'll be good. I'll be good."

"Too late," he said as he smacked her bottom.

Doc stood back and watched the interaction. He couldn't wait until Harper felt safe enough with him to act out on purpose so she could get her bottom reddened. Would she enjoy being spanked in front of people the way Remi did, or would she want it to be kept private? It didn't matter to him either way. He would respect whatever hard limits she had. As long as his girl felt safe within their dynamic, that was all that mattered to him.

Maybe he was getting ahead of himself. They were still just friends. It was what they'd agreed on. But that had been before she'd slept on his chest and let him take care of her. Before she'd called him Daddy. He would have liked to think that even though they didn't know each other very well yet, she could tell he wasn't a threat to her.

His attention snapped back to the present. Remi squirmed and wiggled as Kade reddened her bottom. Doc couldn't help but smile at his friend's handiwork. Her entire bottom was red all the way down to the tops of her thighs. Her plump pussy lips peeked out, glistening with her arousal. Yeah, this was definitely what she'd wanted and needed.

"Are you ready to be a good girl?" Kade asked.

"Yes! I'll be good! I promise," she whimpered.

Kade kept his hand pressed down on her back but stepped out of Doc's way. "I think she's ready to behave, Doc."

He grabbed the lube and thermometer off the sterile tray. "Thanks, Kade. You know the drill, Remi."

She sighed and nodded. Kade slipped a pacifier between her lips and talked quietly to her while Doc spread her bottom cheeks and slathered the thick jelly over her puckered hole.

"Kade, do you want to stretch her a bit?"

Doc had a variety of thermometers to use on the girls, but he always used the thickest one on Remi. He usually had Kade prepare her for it even though the device was only about a half-inch thick.

Kade nodded and reached between her cheeks. Whenever he examined Littles, he never played with them or partook in activities that were more sexual. Unless it had to do with their actual exam, he always left it up to their Daddies.

She let out a moan as Kade dipped his index finger into her bottom, moving it in and out several times.

"She's ready," Kade said, then stepped back to give Doc room.

Slowly, Doc slid the thermometer deep into her bottom. She wiggled a bit but didn't fight him otherwise.

"Setting the timer, Remi. Three minutes," he told her.

She nodded and suckled on her pacifier. Kade stroked her back.

While they waited, Doc grabbed the baby monitor and checked in on Harper. She was sprawled wide open on his bed with the covers kicked off. It worried him that she was still so warm. After he was done with Remi, he'd go and check her temperature again with a forehead thermometer so he wouldn't wake her.

Ding!

"Okay, Little one. You did so good," he praised as he pulled the glass device from her bottom. "No temperature."

She spit out her pacifier. "I told you."

Kade smacked her bottom. *"Princess."*

"Sorry, Daddy," she mumbled.

Doc chuckled. "I'll leave you two alone while I go check on Harper. I think your Little girl wants some more attention."

"I think so too. Her pussy is dripping. I'm not sure if I should let her come, though, since she was so naughty," Kade said with a grin.

The men enjoyed teasing their women with denial, though they never actually denied them for long. Kade was enjoying this as much as Remi was. He loved fulfilling her desires, and Doc was happy he could assist with that.

"I'll be good, Daddy." She was breathless and practically writhing under Kade's hold.

"You better be, princess. Otherwise, I'm going to take you straight back to our suite and put you down for a nap without letting you come first."

"If she starts running a fever, come find me," Doc said before he closed them into the medical room to be alone.

He needed to go check on his own baby girl.

ELEVEN
HARPER

A cold layer of sweat covering her body woke her. When she opened her eyes, she looked around, trying to remember where she was. Her surroundings slowly came into focus as she blinked away the grogginess. Levi's suite.

She let out a sigh of relief and swallowed, wincing from the scratchiness in her throat.

"Ugh," she whimpered.

"Is your throat hurting, baby doll?"

"Oh!" she jolted up. "Oh my God, I didn't see you standing there."

Levi stepped into the room and sat at the edge of the bed. He ran the back of his hand over her forehead.

"Sorry, baby. I didn't mean to scare you," he said gently. "You're still warm. I want to take your temperature again. Is your throat hurting?"

She nodded and winced as she swallowed. "A little."

Levi's brow furrowed with concern as he reached over to the nightstand and grabbed a thermometer.

"I'm sorry you're feeling icky, baby doll," Levi murmured, his voice filled with genuine worry.

Harper's heart fluttered at his tender care, despite her aching body. It felt as though she'd been hit by a train.

"Lie back and roll onto your side," he instructed.

She eyed the thick glass thermometer with a mix of trepidation and arousal. She'd never had her temperature taken in her bottom until today. Heck, she hadn't ever had anyone touch her at all back there. For some reason, it hadn't felt scary having Levi do it. He'd been so gentle and reassuring, and she wanted to please him. She hoped he wouldn't notice the slickness sticking to her thighs.

Levi gently stroked her hair as she shifted onto her side. His touch was comforting, yet there was a hint of anticipation in the air. When he lifted her shirt and tucked his fingers into the back of her panties, she sucked in a breath.

Just like the first time, he treated her with care and was gentle as he parted her cheeks and then spread the thick lube on her bottom hole. When she felt the cold tip of the thermometer, she whimpered softly, but Levi's reassuring words calmed her.

"You're being a good girl, Harper. Daddy is so proud of you. Thank you for trusting me to take care of you."

He pressed the device deep into her bottom. Her nipples puckered, and her pussy ached. She hoped that with the position she was in, he couldn't tell. If he could, he didn't mention it and instead rubbed slow circles on her hip.

"I examined Remi while you were sleeping. She didn't have a fever. I haven't checked on the other Little girls yet, though."

Something tightened in her chest. What did he mean he'd examined Remi? Did he take care of her the same way he had with Harper? Did he touch her bottom hole too? Why was she feeling icky about that?

"Harper." Levi's voice broke through her thoughts.

"Huh?"

He lifted himself so he was hovering over her, his eyebrows furrowed. "What's wrong, baby?"

She shook her head and squeezed her eyes shut then opened them to look at him. "Nothing. I was lost in thought."

His dark eyes pierced hers. "Yeah, I don't think I like what you were thinking about, which means you need to tell me. What was going through your head?"

Thankfully the timer went off, and their conversation was put on the back burner when he pulled the thermometer from her bottom.

"Still over a hundred. I want to look in your throat."

He adjusted her panties over her hips before he took the thermometer into the bathroom and returned a moment later with a small bag in his hand.

"Sit up for me, baby," he instructed.

It was easy to obey. She wanted to please him. To hear the praise he seemed to so easily give.

She expected him to do what he said he was going to do and look in her throat. Instead, he knelt in front of her and cupped her chin.

"Tell Daddy what you were thinking about. I could tell it was hurting you, and I won't allow you to be hurt by anyone, including yourself."

Shoot.

Why wouldn't he let it go? The last thing she wanted to do was admit to being jealous of another woman getting Levi's attention. Jealousy never looked good on anyone.

"Harper, look at me," he said in a firm voice she wasn't used to hearing from him.

She lifted her gaze to meet his and expected to find anger, but she didn't see anything resembling that. Instead, he looked concerned.

"Kitten, the most important thing in a Daddy/Little girl dynamic is open communication and honesty. I will always be open and honest with you. I expect the same in return."

Her shoulders drooped, and her bottom lip trembled. "You'll be mad. Or think I'm crazy."

His eyebrows rose. "First, I won't think you're crazy, and I don't want to hear you talk like that. Second, I won't be mad. If there's something that's bothering you or that you're questioning, I can't make it better if I don't know what it is."

When she didn't respond, he sighed. "Does it have to do with me giving Remi an exam?"

How did he know? Was she that obvious?

"Maybe," she whispered. "Yes. I guess so. It's just that, when you give them exams, do you…do you do the same stuff with them as you do with me?"

Understanding filled his gaze, and he rose to sit on the bed next to her, then pulled her onto his lap. His thick, corded arms held her tightly, and she loved the woodsy scent of his cologne surrounding her.

"When I give the other Little girls exams, their Daddies are always present. I never use my hands or fingers to penetrate them. Only medical tools that are needed for their check-ups."

She stared at the stubble on his chin, trying to absorb what he said. "Do you get turned on?"

His arms tightened, and he pressed a kiss to her temple. "I will always be honest with you. So, the answer is yes. I do. However, it's not that I want to do anything sexual with the other Little girls. I get turned on by the scene. By the power exchange and embarrassment the Littles feel. I get turned on by medical play in general. I love watching my club brothers Daddy their Little girls. But I have no feelings toward them other than platonic ones. The entire time I was with Remi and Kade earlier, all I could think about was how much I couldn't wait until I earned your trust enough to give you the same kind of exams."

Heat spread over her cheeks. She had a feeling he was talking about something much more intimate than having her temperature taken.

"Oh," she murmured. "I'm sorry."

Levi pulled back and cupped her chin. He shook his head. "Don't ever apologize for having insecurities. I want to know when you're unsure of yourself. It's my job to help you feel secure in this relationship."

"We have a relationship?" she asked before she could think better of it.

He smiled and stared at her with so much heat in his gaze, it warmed her whole body.

"I'd sure like us to have a relationship. I can wait, though, if that's what you need. I like you, Harper. I've never believed in love at first sight, but I think I do now."

It felt as though her eyes were going to bug out of her head. "You don't love me."

"Maybe not yet. But I have strong feelings for you. I want to be your Daddy. I want to take care of you and help you heal from the abuse you endured. I want to show you what a loving, respectful relationship should be like. I want it all with you, Little girl. The question is, do you think you could give me a chance to show you?"

Harper's heart pounded in her chest, her mind reeling from Levi's confession. The weight of his words hung in the air, creating a charged silence between them. She searched his eyes, seeking any hint of uncertainty or insincerity, but all she found was unwavering resolve.

Tears welled up in Harper's eyes as she took a shaky breath. It wasn't that she didn't want what Levi was offering. In fact, she wanted it a lot. More than she'd first thought.

"I...I don't know if I'm ready. I'm scared and so damaged from my past relationship," she finally whispered, her voice laced with vulnerability and hesitation.

Levi's thumb gently brushed away a tear that had escaped Harper's eye. His touch was tender, his gaze filled with understanding. "I know you're scared, Little girl," he murmured, his voice soothing and comforting, "but I promise you, I will never hurt you like he did. I will do everything in my power to make sure you feel safe and cared for every single day."

Something in Harper's heart tugged at her, urging her to trust him. She longed for the love he offered, for the safety and security that seemed to radiate from his every touch. But the fear lingered, a constant reminder of the pain she had endured.

Levi leaned in, his lips barely grazing hers. It was a delicate, tender kiss that held so much promise. Harper closed her eyes, allowing herself to enjoy the soft caress of his mouth against hers. In that moment, she made a decision.

With a newfound determination, Harper mustered the strength to speak. "Okay," she said, her voice steady despite the tremor in her heart. "I'll give us a chance."

Her breath caught when a smile bloomed on Levi's face, brightening his eyes. He wrapped his arms around her, enveloping her in a warm embrace. "Thank you," he murmured against her ear. "I promise I won't ever hurt you, baby girl."

A weight lifted from Harper's shoulders. For the first time in a long while, she allowed herself to truly believe there might be a future beyond the pain and darkness of her past.

When he finally released her, he set her on the bed and went about looking in her throat.

"The good news is, I don't think you have strep. I'm pretty sure it's a virus, which means you need lots of rest, fluids, and snuggles from Daddy."

She giggled when he tickled her tummy. Then she frowned. "But I need to go to work. I just started at Dot's. I don't want to let her down."

He raised an eyebrow. "Well, it happens that Dot is my aunt, so I think she'll understand. I'll call her in a bit and explain. She wouldn't want you decorating cakes while you're sick anyway."

Harper supposed he was right. She would hate if she made anyone else sick.

"I want to make sure you don't have any other questions or concerns about me examining the other Littles. You can ask me anything, kitten. I'll never be mad."

Everything he'd said earlier had made sense. She felt a lot better about it, and she was glad they'd talked. It was obvious the other women loved their Daddies whole-heartedly, and the relationship they had with Levi was purely platonic.

"I'm good, Daddy."

The corners of his lips pulled back into a wide grin. "I love it when you call me that. Say it again."

She scrunched her face. "I'm good?"

He let out a low growl. Dang, that was hot. Teasing a man wasn't usually something she would do, but it came easily with Levi.

"Naughty girl."

"You mean, Daddy?"

"You know I mean Daddy. Silly girl. I like hearing it come from you."

Warmth spread through her chest. She liked saying it. It felt as natural as calling someone by their name.

"I need to get you fed, and then it's back to bed for you," he said.

She groaned. She had a feeling he was going to actually put her on bedrest. Something told her Levi wouldn't be letting her lift a finger until she was all better.

"Go potty. Gabriel was making some chili in the main kitchen earlier. I'm going to go grab you a bowl. I'll be right back."

After she used the toilet and washed her hands, Harper looked in the mirror and winced. She looked terrible. Pale and blotchy skin. Her hair was a mess. She had death breath.

Great.

She quickly brushed her teeth and ran her fingers through her tangled locks before she left the bathroom in search of her phone. As soon as she pulled it from her purse, the screen lit up showing multiple calls from unknown numbers. Her stomach tightened as she looked at them. It was possible it was her apartment manager calling with news about when the cleanup would be done. Or the fire department to let her know what caused the fire. Or one of her neighbors calling to check on her. Even though she hadn't given her number to any of them.

Deep down in the pit of her tummy, she knew it wasn't any of those things. It didn't matter, though. She was safe. Levi wouldn't let anything happen to her. Besides, Zach had no idea where she'd moved.

She left her phone on the dresser then climbed into bed and snuggled up under the blankets again. A few minutes later, Levi returned with a steaming bowl of chili. Her clit tightened as he moved toward her. She might be running a fever, but the heat she was feeling had nothing to do with her being sick.

TWELVE
DOC

Seeing Harper in his bed, wrapped up in his blankets, was something he liked. A lot. Even though she'd agreed to give him a chance, he had a long way to go to prove he would never harm her.

He sat down and faced her. When she eyed the bowl in his hands, he held it up and smiled.

"Gabriel made his famous chicken chili. Are you allergic to anything?"

"No. What's so famous about it?"

Doc grinned. "Fuck if I know. I think he calls it that so people think it's extra special. He also has his 'world-famous brownies' and 'award-winning pork chops.' We've never actually seen the award, though, so we're skeptical."

Her soft, melodic giggle filled the room. His chest squeezed. Damn. His friends were right. This Little girl was wrapping him around her precious fingers.

"Open," he commanded softly.

She obeyed, and he fed her spoonful after spoonful, pleased she was eating. It didn't take long before her eyelids started drooping.

"I'm full," she mumbled.

He nodded and set the bowl aside, then shifted so he was resting his back against the headboard. "Come here, baby. I want you to drink a bottle before you go to sleep."

When he wrapped his arms around her and pulled her onto his lap, she snuggled against him. Everything was right in his world. As he held the bottle to her lips, she sucked on it. He loved how natural being a Little seemed to be for her. There was nothing forced about it. She was in her element, and he was too. If only they could stay in their own private bubble for as long as possible.

"I'm going to take care of you, baby girl. Show you what it's supposed to be like to have a Daddy. You're safe with me, Harper."

Their eyes locked. She continued to suckle down the electrolyte juice until her lids dropped closed and her mouth went lax. He pulled the bottle from her lips and set it on the side table. Even though he had a dozen things he could be doing around the clubhouse, he was right where he needed to be.

Her phone started vibrating on the dresser across the room. He flinched at the sound, not wanting it to wake her. As soon as it stopped, he relaxed and tightened his arms around her, letting the warmth of her body soothe him. Just as he started to let his own eyes flutter closed, her phone vibrated again, startling him.

Eyebrows furrowed, he gently shifted her off his lap and settled her onto the mattress. She didn't flinch, and he knew she was sleeping deeply. Hopefully, she'd get the rest she needed to heal quickly.

By the time he rose from the bed, her phone was quiet again. He picked it up and tried to unlock it but was stopped by a passcode request. The last thing he wanted to do was be nosy, but if someone was calling twice in a row, it might be important. It could be her landlord or insurance company. He didn't want to wake her over it, though.

As he went to set the phone down, it started vibrating

again. The caller ID showed unknown number. He glanced at Harper before he took her phone out to the living room and tapped the answer button.

"Hello?"

"Who the fuck is this?" an angry voice demanded.

Every nerve in Doc's body tensed. "Who is *this*?"

The line went dead. He gripped the phone so tightly that he was surprised it didn't crack. It took everything in him not to wake Harper up and ask a million questions. It had to be her ex. Had this asshole been contacting her for a while? Did the other Littles know?

Fuck.

He needed to talk to the guys. The asshole had called from an unknown number. Could it be tracked? Did Harper know where he lived? Because Doc would be happy to go pay the guy a visit and make sure he never contacted her or even whispered her name again.

After peeking in on her to make sure she was still sleeping, he grabbed the baby monitor and took that, along with her phone, to the common room.

Steele was sitting at the dining table with Ivy on his lap while they played a board game with Gabriel and Bear.

"Ivy," Doc said, more roughly than he'd intended.

All eyes went to him, with Ivy on full alert.

"I don't have a fever. Daddy already took my temperature. I don't need an exam," she blurted out.

If he wasn't so pissed, he'd find it adorable how nervous she was about having an exam.

"It's not that. I'm glad you're not sick, though. I need to ask you something," he said as he sat down next to her and Steele.

Ivy nodded, her eyes wide. "Okay. What's wrong? Is Harper okay?"

Doc sighed and set her phone and the monitor on the table. "Did Harper mention anything about her ex? Anything about him still contacting her?"

"What? No. I mean, she told us a little about him, but she didn't say anything about him reaching out to her. Why?"

"I think he called her. From an unknown number. He hung up on me when I asked who it was, but he was definitely pissed that I answered her phone."

Steele furrowed his eyebrows. "Where's Harper?"

"She's asleep. I don't want to wake her. She's been running a fever since the girls came back from their outing today," Doc answered.

"You could call Colt. He might have a way to trace the call," Steele offered.

Colt was a friend of theirs in Seattle. He owned an IT company and could hack anything.

"I'll call him," Doc said. "Until then, we need to be on alert. I don't know if this asshole has a way to track her or not. Keep the girls inside unless one of us is out with them."

Steele nodded. "I'll spread the word. What do you need from us?"

Doc shrugged. "I don't know yet. It's possible it wasn't him. The way he spoke to me, though, tells me it is."

Bear sat up straighter and nodded toward the hallway. Doc turned and watched Harper sleepily shuffle toward him. He stood and opened his arms for her.

"Hey, kitten," he said as he hugged her to his chest.

"Is it okay that I came out here?" she whispered.

He furrowed his eyebrows and cupped her chin so he could look her square in the eye. "Absolutely, baby girl. You can go anywhere in the clubhouse you want except for private suites. Did you start feeling worse?"

She shook her head, her cheeks turning pink. "I had to go potty. I actually feel a lot better."

He held his hand over her forehead and breathed a sigh of relief. "Your fever is gone. It might have been a reaction from the smoke inhalation you had. Your body might be trying to fight off something."

"I hope so. I don't like being sick. It's the worst."

"It is the worst. Although, I do like taking care of my Little girl when she's not feeling well."

The way her cheeks kept turning pink was so adorable. She couldn't mask her emotions if she tried. It was precious. Nothing about his girl was fake or forced. She was truly a Little girl at heart. His Little girl. His to protect. Shit. He had to ask her about the man who called her.

"I need to talk to you," he said as he picked her up and settled her on his hip.

He sat on one of the couches and wrapped his arms around her, loving the way she snuggled right into his chest.

"Baby, while you were sleeping, your phone kept ringing, so I answered it. It was an unknown number, and it was a man on the line. He seemed pretty angry. Do you know who it might be?"

Her gaze immediately dropped to her lap as her bottom lip trembled. When she looked up at him, and he saw tears in her eyes, it felt as though his chest was cracking right down the center.

"I'm pretty sure it's my ex. He's messaged me a couple of times from unknown numbers, and each time I block them. I don't know why he won't leave me alone."

Fuck. He was going to find this guy and kill him.

Tears streamed down her face. The urge to kill that asshole turned into an urge to torture him first.

"Okay, baby girl. It's gonna be okay. Daddy's got you," he crooned, running his hand over her hair.

Ivy approached them, her own lips trembling as she sat down and grabbed Harper's hand. "They won't let anything happen to you. You're safe with us."

Harper pulled her head away from his chest and looked up at him with the saddest eyes. "I'm sorry I didn't tell you."

Doc shook his head. "It's okay, baby girl. You're still learning to trust me. Going forward, though, I need you to tell me things like this. It's a rule in this club. If anything ever happens, you tell me immediately, and if I'm not around, you find one of the other guys and tell them. We'll do everything we can to protect you, but we can't if we don't know what's going on. Understand?"

"Yes. I understand. I'm sorry," she said, sniffling.

"Does he know where you live, baby?"

She shook her head. "No. I don't think so."

He was glad she hadn't given him her new address, but he was also smart enough to know that finding that kind of information wasn't impossible.

"What if he comes after me?" she asked in a trembling voice.

Doc shook his head. "You're part of the Guardians now. We'll protect you."

He meant it. He and his MC brothers would do whatever was needed to protect her and any other Little who belonged to them.

King entered the room, his eyes dark with rage. As soon as he laid eyes on Harper, his expression softened slightly. "Doc, can I see you for a minute?"

Steele rose from the table and moved over to the couch. "I'll sit with Harper and Ivy."

Harper nibbled on her bottom lip, her eyes wide as she looked Steele up and down. The man was intimidating. Especially to people who didn't know him well. Doc knew she was safe with him, though. Steele was putty for all the Littles in the house.

"You'll be fine. Ivy will stay and hang out with you too. I'll be right back."

She glanced at Steele one more time before she nodded. "Okay, Daddy," she replied so quietly only he could hear.

His heart pounded and his cock ached when she called him Daddy. As much as he wanted to move slowly with her, his body felt differently. He wanted to take her back to his suite, strip off all her clothes, and show her exactly how perfect she was. Show her how a real man treated a woman.

When she shifted on his lap, her eyes widened, and he groaned inwardly. He could control a lot of things, but the way his body reacted to her was not one of them. She was definitely feeling the way his cock had thickened for her.

"Sorry, baby girl. Ignore it. I can't help the way you make me feel," he whispered.

The corners of her mouth tipped up, and she moved her bottom against him again. He gripped her hips to still her before he embarrassed himself right in the middle of the clubhouse.

"Stop it, naughty girl. Be good. We'll be right back."

Before she could react, he lifted her off his lap and set her on the couch next to Ivy. King led him down the hall until they were far enough away they wouldn't be heard.

"What's up, man?" Doc asked.

"I was just down at the firehouse. Chief said the fire at Harper's complex was arson. A witness told the police they saw a man, who looked to be in his thirties, running away from the building right before it went up in flames."

Doc froze, every bit of air rushing from his lungs. It was him. Her ex.

"It gets worse," King told him. "The fire was actually set on her side of the apartment. Someone used an accelerant to start the fire in her garbage can out the back. Instead of catching her side on fire, it caught the neighbor's ivy on fire and burned that side. Her back window was open, though, which is why it got so smoky in there."

Doc started breathing heavily, unable to believe what he was hearing.

King sighed and ran a hand over his hair. "It also appears someone was in Harper's apartment before the fire. The smoke detectors in her place had been removed, and the lock on her back door was mangled like someone used a knife to break it."

"What?" Doc shouted.

King sighed. "I'm sorry, man. I wish I had better news."

"He tried to kill her. If she hadn't woken up from the smoke, she would have died in that fire," Doc ground out.

He could have lost her. That thought made his chest tighten and his stomach turn. Her ex was going to pay dearly. It was only a matter of time.

THIRTEEN
HARPER

As soon as Levi and King came back to the community room, she knew something was wrong. Both men looked pissed, and immediately, all the other men in the room went on alert.

"What's going on?" Steele asked.

"I need to talk to Harper. King will fill you guys in," Levi replied as he picked her up.

She clung to him and wrapped her legs around his waist. His body was rigid and his movements harsh as he carried her back to his suite.

"Daddy, what's wrong?"

Fear started to wrap itself around her, and her breathing quickened. Whatever King had told him was bad. Very bad.

After he closed the door behind him, Levi took her to the couch and set her down, then knelt on the floor in front of her.

"Baby, I need to tell you something. It's going to be scary, but you need to remember you're safe with me."

Her body started to tremble, and she couldn't catch her breath. "What is it?"

"The fire was arson," he said quietly.

For some reason, she didn't think that was the worst of what he had to tell her.

"It appears someone was in your apartment before the fire. The smoke detectors had been removed, and the lock on your door had been messed with."

A sob caught in her throat. "But...but, I was there. I was in my apartment. How? I would have heard someone, right? How could this happen?"

"I need to know where he lives."

Her eyes widened. "Why? What are you going to do?"

The rage she saw burning in his dark eyes didn't scare her. It made her feel safer than she'd ever felt before, but the last thing she wanted was for him to get hurt. Or do something to get arrested.

"I need the address, Harper," he said sternly.

She reached out and pressed her palms against his chest. "Daddy—"

"Harper, this isn't negotiable. I'll let you argue with me on a lot of things, but when it comes to your safety, I have no give. As your Daddy, it's my job to protect you, and I will do it by whatever means necessary."

Emotions whirled in her chest. Arousal. Fear. Anger. Awe.

Levi hardly knew her, yet he was willing to do whatever it took to protect her. He was willing to fight the demon who'd made her life hell for so long.

"Okay. I'll give you his address," she whispered.

His shoulders relaxed as he nodded. "That's my good girl."

She sighed at his praise. It was still so foreign. Feeling a sliver of boldness, she reached up and ran her fingers over his rough chin. He kept his eyes locked on hers, but he was breathing heavily. Like he was fighting to keep control. It was an empowering feeling.

"Harper."

"Daddy," she whispered.

And then his mouth was on hers, kissing her as if his next

breath depended on it. His hand cupped the back of her head, holding her firmly in place. She wrapped her arms around his shoulders and moaned into his mouth. There was something about this moment that felt electrified. Smoldering. Intimate. Maybe it was because he was so forceful about wanting to protect her. Whatever it was, she was turned on, and she wanted him.

When she parted her lips to let him in, he took the invitation and explored her mouth, leaving her breathless. Not wanting things to stop, she gripped his shirt and tried to tug him back to her, but he shook his head.

"I don't want to stop, either," he said. "But you haven't been feeling well, and I need to go."

"I'm feeling better," she whined.

She knew she sounded like a brat, but she might combust if they didn't keep going. Her core ached, her breasts felt heavy and sensitive, and the bulge she saw in his pants was practically making her drool.

The stern look he pinned her with did nothing to cool her down. Instead, it turned her on more. She'd never thought of herself as being a brat, but the urge to have a small tantrum was right there.

"I'm glad you feel better, but you still need to rest. I want this as badly as you do," he said, grabbing his bulge with a groan. "Maybe more. But I won't ever put your health at risk for pleasure."

She let out a dramatic sigh. "Fiiiine."

"I like your sassy side, kitten. I look forward to spanking your adorable bottom when you get a little too sassy with me."

A shiver ran through her. His words were doing nothing to tamp down her arousal. She wanted Levi to spank her. She had no doubt being bent over his thighs would make her feel so incredibly Little. She also knew he wouldn't harm her.

"Go potty. I'm going to go make you something to eat. Then you're going back to bed."

Another sigh, and she nodded. "Okay."

He leaned forward and kissed her again. "My good girl."

When he left her alone, she went to the bathroom and did her business. She was feeling a lot better, but being tucked into bed to rest did sound nice. Maybe he would let her watch a movie.

She didn't know what to think about him going to talk to Zach. What was he going to say? What if it hadn't been Zach who started the fire? She wanted to believe the man she spent years with wouldn't try to kill her. Then again, he had told her a number of times he'd kill her if she ever left him. It was one of the reasons she'd stayed for so long.

Levi was sitting on the bed when she came out of the bathroom. Her mouth went dry when he smiled at her. Gosh, he was hot. And even better, he was good. The things her new friends had told her about him helped, but deep down in her soul, she knew it was actually true. He wouldn't hurt her. Levi was the type of man who would hurt himself before he ever hurt a woman. Getting knocked over by that other motorcycle club had sucked, but she was half tempted to send them a thank you card since she got to meet her new Daddy because of them.

"Come sit," he said.

She moved over to him, but before she could sit next to him, Levi pulled her onto his lap. He was so big compared to her. It was easy to fall into Little Space around him. Partially because she knew she was safe to be there.

"How do chicken nuggets sound?"

Her eyes lit up as she bobbed her head. "My favorite."

He chuckled. "Why doesn't that shock me?"

Just like he had with the soup, he hand-fed her each bite. When she was finally too full to eat any more, she shook her head and rubbed her tummy.

"Crawl into bed, baby."

She climbed under the covers, and Levi handed her Whiskers, then started tucking the blankets around her.

"What are you going to say to him?" she asked, suddenly anxious.

He grunted and met her gaze. "Everything he needs to know to understand not to fuck with what's mine."

For some reason, she was pretty sure Levi wouldn't be doing much talking when he paid Zach a visit.

"Will you take someone with you?"

It wasn't that she didn't think Levi could take care of himself. She didn't want anything to happen to him. He was growing on her. A lot. Zach was smaller than him, but he was also completely unhinged.

"Yes, baby. I'll take a few guys with me."

She let herself relax. He'd be fine.

He leaned over and pressed a kiss to her forehead. "Stay in bed. I'm going to turn on the baby monitor and give the receiver to Gabriel. If you need anything while I'm gone, just call out for him, and he'll come check on you. Okay?"

She rolled her lips in and nodded. The last thing she would do would be to bother Gabriel with anything. He seemed nice enough, but he wasn't her Daddy. She didn't want to be annoying.

"I mean it, Little girl. We all do our part in taking care of the Littles in this club. And since I go on three-day shifts at the firehouse, you're going to have to get used to having babysitters."

Her mouth dropped open. "I don't need babysitters."

"You're my baby, so when I'm on shift, you will have my brothers watching over you. No arguments. My job is to keep you safe, protected, and cared for. I'll do whatever it takes to take care of my girl."

The hard set of his expression told her it was pointless to argue. Levi was soft about a lot of things with her, but it seemed when it came to her safety or health, he wouldn't budge.

"Hurry back?" she asked.

He nodded and pressed a kiss to her lips. "I'll be home as soon as I can. I'll miss you, Little one."

"I'll miss you too, Daddy."

FOURTEEN
DOC

"Who's available to take a ride with me to go have a chat with Harper's ex?"

King, Kade, Storm, Bear, Steele, and Atlas all perked up.

"We're game," King said darkly.

Storm nodded, his scowl deepening. "Definitely game. I have a few words to say to the guy too."

Doc grinned and looked at Gabriel. "You mind watching the girls?"

Gabriel smiled. "Not at all. You Little girls want to watch a movie?"

The excitement the girls showed over something so simple made Doc feel warm inside. He wished Harper were well enough to hang out with them, but she needed to rest. Even if she was feeling better, her body was obviously fighting something, or she wouldn't have had a fever earlier.

"Here's the baby monitor. Harper's in bed watching a movie. I told her she needed to rest, but if she needed anything to call out for you."

"Of course. Want me to check on her in a bit?" Gabriel asked.

"That would be great. I'll text her and let her know. Call or text me if anything comes up."

"You got it," Gabriel answered.

Doc led his brothers out of the clubhouse, and together, they rode through the streets of Shadowridge to the next town over. His body vibrated with rage the entire time. This motherfucker had set her apartment on fire. He'd been in her home while she was asleep. He'd hurt her and tried to kill her. This wasn't going to end well for him. Not at all. He'd be lucky if he could walk after Doc finished with him.

Forty-five minutes later, they pulled up to a two-story house in a neat little suburb. The home was pristine all the way down to the perfectly painted mailbox out front. It made his rage burn hotter. Everything about this fucker's house screamed normal. Screamed money. Doc would bet his last dollar that the neighbors had no idea what that fucker was doing to Harper behind closed doors.

They parked down the road, wanting to keep the noise of their bikes from alerting him to their arrival. It would be fun to chase him. A little cat-and-mouse game where Doc scared the piss out of the guy. But what was more important to Doc was getting back to his baby girl and starting their life together.

As they made their way down the sidewalk, the energy that surrounded them was thick with tension. Storm cracked his knuckles while King punched the air a couple of times as though he were getting ready for a big fight. Doc grinned. His brothers barely knew Harper. She meant nothing to them. But because she meant something to him, they considered her family, and the Guardians took care of their family.

When they were halfway up the walkway, they heard a woman scream. All at once, they froze.

"Did you hear that?" Steele asked.

Doc nodded. "Yeah. Was that coming from inside the house?"

Another scream confirmed it, and they took off running.

Doc pounded on the front door. If they had to, they'd break it down. The last thing he wanted was a breaking and entering charge, but if that woman screamed again, he'd kick it in without a second thought.

The door swung open, and Doc found himself standing face to face with the man who'd hurt his Little girl.

"What?" Zach asked.

A woman with red-rimmed eyes cowered behind him, holding one of her arms close to her chest. She was shaking like a leaf. All it took was one glance at the woman to know Zach was hurting her the same way he'd hurt Harper.

Without a word, Doc pulled his fist back and smashed it into his face. The hit caught Zach off guard, causing him to stumble back. Blood trickled from the fucker's nose as he clutched his face, disbelief etched across his features. Doc stood tall, his chest heaving.

Zach regained his footing, his expression shifting to rage. He lunged, but Doc had anticipated the move and sidestepped the attack effortlessly. Instead, Zach ended up in the grasp of Bear and Steele.

As Zach struggled against Bear's grip, his face contorted with anger. His attempts to break free were fruitless. Doc gripped Zach's throat, squeezing hard enough to make the man's eyes bulge.

"You hurt my girl. You tried to kill her," Doc ground out.

Zach's eyes darkened. He sputtered for a few seconds until Doc released his neck.

"That fucking whore. Ungrateful little bitch," he shouted.

Doc saw red and threw another punch to Zach's stomach, causing him to double over in pain. The hold Steele and Bear had on him stopped him from being able to move very far.

Doc stepped closer until he was only inches from Zach's face. "You set her apartment on fire. You broke in and removed her smoke detectors. You tried to murder her!"

His shouts echoed down the street, but he didn't care. The

neighbors needed to know what kind of piece of shit they'd been living next to.

Zach was practically foaming from the mouth as he scowled at Doc. "Fuck you, man! She fucking deserved it! She should have died in that fire. No one leaves me!"

The woman who was still standing in the doorway started crying. Kade stepped over to her and comforted her.

A sinister smile spread across Doc's lips as he pulled his fist back and clocked the guy in the face again. Blood dripped from his mouth in a satisfying red stream onto his white shirt.

"How could you try to kill an innocent woman?" Doc snarled.

Zach spat, his blood landing on Doc's cut. Thank fuck it was leather and could be easily cleaned.

"She's not innocent. She left me. She lied to me and left me. Now she's whoring around with you! She deserves to die."

This time it was Storm who punched him with a satisfying crunch. Zach screamed in pain.

"I'll kill you all! You're dead! She's dead!" he shouted.

With a smirk, Doc pulled a small recording device from his front pocket and held it up.

"And you're going to jail for a long, long time. King, call the cops."

Zach started struggling, trying to get free, kicking and screaming against the hold Bear and Steele had on him. Neighbors had started coming out of their houses, watching the commotion.

"She's going to press charges," Kade announced.

Doc's smile widened. "Good. Both women will get justice. Although, I'd say attempted murder alone is going to put him away for a long, long time."

"The police aren't going to believe you thugs! You're biker trash! You came to my house and beat me up. You'll go to jail for assault!" Zach shouted.

The men all started laughing.

"From what we saw, you swung at them first," a man called out from behind them.

They turned to find a couple standing at the end of the walkway. Doc raised an eyebrow. That was definitely not how it had gone down. Not that he cared. He'd take an assault charge. If it meant protecting his girl and this other woman, it was well worth it.

"We had a feeling you were hurting poor Harper, but whenever we tried to talk to her, she avoided us," the man said. "Now you're trying to beat up these fine men who came to save this new woman you're abusing. Shame on you."

Doc grinned. These neighbors were about to be his new best friends.

"Fuck you!" Zach screamed.

"No, man. Fuck you. You're a coward. I can't wait until someone makes you their bitch in prison, because there's no doubt in my mind that will happen," Storm growled.

Sirens approached. The next hour was spent answering questions, turning over the recording of Zach's confession, and thanking the neighbors for their help. Kade called the woman's brother to come get her. Once she left with him, they made their way back to their bikes.

Doc grabbed a towel from his saddlebag and wiped the blood from his hands.

Bear grinned. "The look on his face when you pulled out the recorder. I think he pissed himself."

All of them burst out laughing.

"Come on. Let's get back to our girls," Kade said. "I feel like I need to hold Remi a little tighter tonight."

Without another word, they all climbed onto their bikes and headed toward the compound.

FIFTEEN
HARPER

Warmth surrounded her, along with the scents of citrus and leather. She opened her eyes and found her Daddy lying in bed next to her with his head propped up on his hand. He was watching her.

"Hi, kitten," he murmured.

She let her pacifier fall from her lips. "Hi, Daddy."

"I didn't mean to wake you. I just…I needed to see you for a bit before I went to sleep."

He was freshly showered and shirtless, and holy crap, he smelled delicious. His dark hair was still wet and combed away from his face.

"I'm glad you woke me," she whispered.

When he reached up to brush a stray hair away from her face, she noticed the bandages on his hand and sucked in a breath.

"You got hurt?" she asked, her bottom lip trembling.

He quickly pulled his hand away and shook his head. "I'm not hurt. My knuckles are a little messed up, but they'll heal quickly. He's in a lot worse condition than me."

"What happened? When do I have to talk to the police?"

Levi stroked her tummy and smiled. "Probably within the

next few days. He admitted to it, and I recorded it, so he's already been arrested. He won't be coming for you anymore. You're safe, baby."

Tears dripped from her eyes as a sob broke free. She was safe. Zach couldn't hurt her anymore. She could finally live her life without fear.

"Fuck, baby, I didn't mean to make you cry," he murmured as he brushed the tears away.

She threw her arms around his neck and sobbed louder. "They're happy tears. Thank you, Daddy. Thank you."

"I'd do anything for you, baby. Anything. You're mine. I take that seriously."

They clung to each other. It wasn't until she started dozing off in his embrace that he pulled away.

"You need to go to sleep, baby. I'm going to go out to the couch."

Her eyes widened. "No. Please. Please stay with me. I don't want you to go."

He stared at her for a long moment before he sighed. "I'm afraid of having a nightmare with you in bed next to me. I don't want to frighten you."

"You won't, Levi. I trust you, and I know you'll never hurt me. I want to be there with you if you wake up to a bad dream. I want to be there to comfort you like you always do for me."

His eyes turned glassy as he swallowed several times. Finally, he nodded. "Okay. If you're sure," he said roughly.

"I'm sure, Daddy. I've never felt so sure."

"Me either, baby."

After he climbed under the covers with her, he picked up her pacifier and slid it between her lips. She was shy at first, but when he stared down at her with nothing but adoration, she relaxed and snuggled into his chest, feeling happier than she could ever remember being.

"Night, my baby," he whispered.

She closed her eyes and sighed, letting herself slip into dreamland.

Something hard pressed into her back. It took her a few seconds to pull out of the deep sleep she'd been in all night. As soon as her eyes fluttered open and she took in her surroundings, her lips spread into a slow smile. She was safe. With her Daddy. And she knew exactly what the hardness was. Unable to help herself, she wiggled her hips and sucked in a breath. It was huge. Long and definitely thick from what she could feel through their clothes.

When she scooted back a little farther, Levi's warm hand landed on her hip, making her squeal in surprise.

"Are you trying to torture me, kitten?" His voice was deep and raspy from sleep.

"I didn't know you were awake."

He chuckled and pressed a kiss to her neck. "I've been awake and watching you for the past hour. How's my girl?"

Horny. That's how. She wasn't about to say it out loud, though.

"Better. I slept like a rock."

His hand started trailing up her side. "I did too. Best sleep I've had in a long time."

"No nightmares?"

"No nightmares," he confirmed.

Her insides warmed. It had only been one night, but she hoped maybe she could be like his own personal stuffie and keep him from having bad dreams. It was probably silly, but she hated the thought of the most wonderful man she'd ever met going through that.

He kissed her neck again, his stubble tickling the sensitive skin. She giggled and squirmed, her bottom pushing up against his cock. He let out a low growl and rolled her toward him so she was on her back. He lowered his gaze to her pebbled nipples, then licked his bottom lip.

He reached out and cupped her chin, bringing her face to his. As soon as his mouth captured hers, it was like neither of them could get enough as they started clawing at each other. A hand moved over her breast, molding to the sensitive mound.

The bulge she'd felt pressing against her bottom minutes ago had started the fire within her, and all she could think about was how much she wanted him. Her Daddy. The man who was showing her that not all men were like her ex. Not all men were abusive and mean.

His thumb brushed over her nipple, and even through the thin top, it sent a jolt of electricity through her.

"Daddy," she whimpered against his lips.

"I know, baby. I know," he murmured.

"Please."

He pulled his mouth away from hers and stared into her eyes as if he were thinking something through.

"Once I take you, Harper, you're mine. Are you sure you want that?"

"I thought I was already yours. So, make me feel it. *Please*, Daddy. Don't make me beg."

His lips pulled into a smirk. "I might like the thought of you begging, Little girl."

She giggled but was quickly cut off by his mouth capturing hers again as he gripped her hips and moved over her. She spread her thighs apart until his bulge pressed against her core. It felt big. Really big.

He stroked her nipple again before moving his hand to the other breast.

The intensity of it all built within her. Her heart raced as he played with her nipples, sending shivers down her spine.

"Please, Daddy, take me now," she pleaded, her voice barely more than a whisper.

"No, not yet. I have other ways to bring my Little girl to her peak." He slowly trailed his fingers down her abdomen, teasing her sensitive skin and leaving a trail of electricity as he went. She got wetter by the second, aching for his touch. His fingers reached the edge of her panties.

"Do you want me to stop, Little girl?" he asked.

She shook her head, keeping her gaze on his. "No, Daddy. Please don't stop. I need you."

His hand slid lower into her panties until the rough pad of his finger pressed against the sensitive button, which had her bucking her hips toward him.

"So responsive, baby. So fucking wet."

When he circled her clit, she cried out. He leaned down to capture her moan with his mouth. She raked her fingernails over his chest. He pulled his hand away from her clit, and she couldn't stop the whimper of protest that escaped.

"So needy, baby," he said with a smirk.

The only thing she did was bob her head. She let her gaze roam over his muscular chest, following the lines of all the ink covering his body.

When he reached out and yanked her top up and over her head, she yelped in surprise. Her nipples ached for his touch.

As if he could read her mind, he leaned forward and captured one of them in his mouth, sucking roughly as he tugged her panties off.

He pulled away and ran his gaze over her body. She started to doubt herself, but when his gaze met hers, she saw nothing but lust for her in his dark irises.

"You're beautiful," he murmured.

"Thank you, Daddy," she whispered.

"Spread your legs wide for me. I want to see your pretty pussy."

Her heart fluttered as she slowly opened her thighs. As

soon as he looked down at her mound, he groaned and gripped his cock through his underwear.

When he started lowering his boxer briefs, she sucked in a breath and let it out as his cock sprang free. Thick and long, it hung heavy between his legs. She'd seen porn before, but she wasn't sure the men in those videos measured up to Levi.

When his fingers ran along the seam of her pussy, she whimpered and flexed her hips, trying to get more friction. Using his thumb, he flicked her clit and rubbed circles around it until she was moaning and crying out for him.

"Please. I need you. I need to feel you," she begged.

Levi's gaze never left her as he began to stroke his thick member, the tip glistening with pre-cum. She could see his breathing quicken, and her own desire swelled within her.

Gently, Levi placed his hands on her inner thighs, spreading them wider. With a deep breath, he moved closer, the heat radiating from his body. He reached toward the nightstand and dug through the top drawer. The sound of a condom wrapper crinkled. A second later, she watched him roll the rubber down his length. Why was that so hot?

"Who do you belong to, Harper?"

Her heart swelled. "You."

He nodded. "That's right, baby. You belong to me. You know what that means?"

She shook her head.

As his cock nudged against her swollen lips, she gasped at the sensation.

"It means you're mine to take care of. Mine to protect. Mine to show what it's like to be loved."

Levi held her gaze, searching for approval in her expression.

"I'm yours," she confirmed.

His hands gripped her hips tightly, his breath coming in ragged gasps as he pressed into her.

"Oh, fuck, you're so tight," he whispered.

She cried out in pleasure, her own hands instinctively clawing at his back as she rose to meet his every thrust. His arms rested on either side of her face, forcing her to stare up at him.

It was so much. She was so full, almost painfully so, but that only added to the pleasure of it all.

"More. I need more."

Levi planted his palms on the bed and lifted his upper body as he thrust deeper. He started slowly, but it didn't take long before he was fucking her hard and rough. She cried out as she gripped the bedding beside her. Her orgasm close.

"Mine," he ground out.

"Yes! Yours!" she moaned.

Using one hand to keep himself held up, he moved his other to her clit. Her legs started to shake as her climax began to explode.

"That's it, baby. Come for Daddy. Come for me, Little one."

She screamed and bucked her hips against his, clawing at his chest while her pussy pulsed around him. Suddenly, he started thrusting harder and faster until he was grunting out his own orgasm.

As soon as they both quieted, he lowered himself so his entire body was hovering over her with their mouths only inches apart. She wrapped her arms around his neck and sighed. That was an experience. A hot one. Definitely something she would be dreaming about for a very long time.

Sex with her ex had never felt like that. He had never made her come. It had been all about him and his needs. Levi was so different. Every single thing with Levi was different. Better. Hotter. Softer. Safer. And she hoped he'd meant it about never letting her go because she was pretty sure she'd found the Daddy she'd always wished for.

SIXTEEN
DOC

After taking a minute in the bathroom to clean up, he grabbed a washcloth and ran it under the hot water. Then he took it into the bedroom and smiled when he saw that Harper hadn't budged from where he'd left her. Her arm was thrown over her face, and he wondered if she'd fallen asleep. When he gently lowered the cloth to her pussy, she yelped and tried to sit up.

"Shh. It's okay. Daddy's just cleaning you up.

As soon as he finished, he scooped her up from the bed and carried her into the bathroom. When he set her down in front of the toilet, she looked up at him with uncertainty.

"Sit down and go potty. I'll wipe you when you're done."

Her eyes practically bugged out. All of this was new to her, and it would take time for her to get used to him taking care of her in such intimate ways. She would learn quickly he was that kind of Daddy. Even if it embarrassed her, he loved being able to care for her in such basic ways.

"Sit," he said with a raised brow.

After a few seconds of staring at him, she finally lowered herself to the toilet. "Can I have some privacy?" Her cheeks were pink, but her pupils were blown wide, and her nipples were puckering all over again. She might be asking for privacy, but her body was telling him that wasn't truly what she wanted.

"No. Unless you use your safeword, I'm staying right here to watch over you. Now, go potty."

He leaned against the vanity across from the toilet and crossed his arms over his chest. His cock started to throb again, and he was glad he'd slipped on a pair of boxers when he'd gotten up. He wasn't sure how she'd react to him getting hard over watching her use the toilet. Maybe he was a sick fuck, but he wasn't going to hide who he was. Unless she used her safeword, he was the one in charge.

After a few seconds, he heard the trickle hitting the water, and he felt a surge of pride within him.

"Good girl," he crooned when she finished.

When he reached for the toilet paper, her eyes widened again.

"I can do it," she insisted.

He paused and cupped her chin so she was forced to look at him. "I know you can do it. But I want to do it. I love being a Daddy and being able to take care of you. This is how it will be between us all the time. Your only job is to be my Little girl and follow the rules I have in place. Understand?"

She shivered and sucked in a breath but then nodded. "Okay, Daddy."

After quickly wiping her clean, he lifted her off the toilet, and then washed his hands before he led her into the bedroom. He found some clothes for her and made a mental note to order some more so she had plenty of Little and big girl clothes to choose from while she was at the clubhouse. Although, he was already trying to figure out how to convince her to move in with him so he could watch over her all the time. The last thing he wanted to do was scare her by moving too quickly, though.

"Hungry?" he asked as he tugged one of his T-shirts over her head.

"Yes. Do you think Bear is making pancakes again?"

His chest expanded, and he felt warm all over. She was going to fit in perfectly in this house.

"I'm sure he is. He makes them most mornings."

When she lifted up onto her tiptoes and clapped her hands, he nearly exploded with happiness. She was so damn adorable and perfect for him. The Little girl he'd always dreamed of but never thought he'd find.

Hand in hand, they went out to the community room where Harper was immediately swarmed by the other Littles.

"You're okay!" Remi squealed.

"We missed you," Ivy practically yelled.

"You just had sex!" Carlee said.

Harper's cheeks turned bright red. Atlas walked up behind Carlee and swatted her bottom. "Little girl, you're in big trouble."

Carlee's mouth fell open. "Why?"

Atlas sighed and pressed his fingers to the bridge of his nose. "You girls might talk about that sort of thing in private but announcing it in front of everyone is rude. You embarrassed your friend. Apologize, *now*."

Carlee's entire face fell as she looked at Harper, and Doc felt a little bad for her. She looked completely crushed that she might have embarrassed his Little girl.

"I'm so sorry, Harper," she said.

Harper grinned and accepted the hug that Carlee was offering. "It's okay. We totally just had sex. It was great."

Doc choked while Atlas burst out laughing.

"Apparently, we do announce it," Doc said as tears leaked from the corners of his eyes.

Carlee and Harper looked up at both the men and shrugged before they grabbed each other's hands and headed toward the kitchen where Bear was flipping pancakes.

Atlas gave Doc a back-slapping hug. "I'm happy for you, man. She's a sweet Little girl. She fits in perfect with us."

"She really does. I'm a lucky bastard, and I'll never forget it."

Soft curves wiggled under his fingertips. When he opened his eyes, he found his girl curled up in his hold with a book in her hand. It was the fourth night they'd slept in the same bed together, and the second day he'd slept longer than Harper. In that time, he hadn't had a single nightmare.

"Hey, baby girl."

She dropped the book and rolled back to look up at him, a smile playing on her lips. "Hi, Daddy. You were snoring like a freight train."

His eyes widened as heat crept up his face. "Seriously? I never snore." How embarrassing. He hoped he hadn't kept her awake.

She burst out giggling. "No. Not really."

"Why you little…" he said as he tickled her sides.

She kicked and squealed, trying to get free. By the time he gave her mercy, he was on top of her, pressing his cock against her core.

"Sorry, Daddy," she giggled. "It's just fun to mess with you. I never felt safe to do that until I met you."

All the laughter slid off his face. He stared down at her, his gaze locked with hers as he lowered his mouth and captured her lips. She moaned into the kiss and whimpered as she wrapped her arms around his shoulders. When he pulled back, they both smiled.

"You can mess with me as much as you want, baby girl. You're always safe with me. You might get your cute little bottom spanked for being a brat once in a while, but I'll never hurt you. I love your playful side."

Her smile was so bright and genuine, his heart squeezed in his chest. It might take a while, but this Little girl was already blossoming under his care.

"I love you, Harper."

Tears filled her eyes as she let out a sob. "I love you too, Daddy."

He brushed the tears away, then leaned down and kissed her on each temple. She was perfect for him. In every way. She was healing his hurts as much as he was healing hers.

"Move in with me," he whispered.

She blinked several times as she gazed up at him, her lips parted like she was trying to think of what to say.

"If it's too soon, I understand. I'll wait as long as you need," he added.

When she still didn't say anything, he started to worry he'd gone too far. Pushed her too hard. The last thing he wanted to do was scare her or back her into a corner. That hadn't been his intention at all.

"I...I would like that," she said quietly. "I'm scared, though. What if I become too much for you? Or I'm too needy? I struggle with making decisions, and I'm insecure, and often scared of things most people wouldn't think twice about. I might be too much work."

Anger coursed through him. Not at her. No. Never at her. At the asshole who made her feel like she was nothing. Doc wanted to go find that fucker again and punch him a few more times.

He gently cupped her face. "Baby girl, you're never too much for me. As far as making decisions, I would love for you to allow me to do that part for you. I love being in control and being able to pick your clothes, or pick your meals, or whatever else you struggle with. That would make me so happy. Everyone has insecurities. Even me. So, when you're unsure or worried, I want you to come and talk to me. To let me reassure you about my feelings and intentions for you. There's no possible way you could be too needy for me. I want to be needed. It's the Daddy in me."

She searched his face for a moment before she finally nodded. "Let's do it. I want to move in with you."

"We can go as slow as you need, baby. If you want to keep your apartment for a while until you feel comfortable letting it go, we can do that. I want you to be totally sure."

"I'm sure," she said firmly. "I want this. I don't know how, but I know I'm meant to be yours, and I want to be with you as much as possible. But, what about when you have to go to work? Surely all the other guys won't want me hanging around the clubhouse."

He raised an eyebrow. "Why wouldn't they? You're one of us now. Part of this family. They're all as protective as me, and I know they already adore you. We all watch out for each other here, and that includes the women in our lives. So yeah, they'll want you here, baby."

"Oh. Okay. And there's always other Littles here?" she asked.

"Yep."

"Oh, goody. So, I'll have other Littles to play with," she squealed.

Doc laughed and nodded. "Yeah, baby. You'll have all kinds of people who love you here. We're a big family, and you're part of that now."

SEVENTEEN
HARPER

The lump in her throat was so big, it was hard to swallow. She was part of their family. Levi's family. It had been so long since she'd felt like she belonged anywhere. It was a new and exciting feeling. A bit scary too. Scary in a good way, though.

"Come on, baby. I need to get you dressed and ready for the day. Then breakfast before work."

It was her first day back at work since the fire. Thankfully, Dot had been super understanding about the whole situation. She had also been thrilled to find out her nephew had someone special.

She groaned, and he chuckled. "You don't have to work if you don't want to, baby."

Her eyes widened as she looked at him. "What? No, I want to work. I love my job, and Dot is so wonderful. I just hate the thought of leaving you."

Something hard throbbed against her core, and she instantly widened her thighs so he could get closer.

"I hate the thought of being away from you too. If I could, I'd put you in my pocket and keep you there forever. That way no other man could ever lay eyes on you, and I could always keep you safe."

His possessiveness was so hot. It turned her on how much he wanted her. He never tried to hide it, either. If they were in the same room together, his hands were pretty much always on her. It made her feel sexy and desired.

"We have a little time," she whimpered.

"We do. So, what am I going to do with my Little girl in that time?" he asked, flexing his hips toward her.

Before she could answer, his mouth was on hers as they started clawing at each other to remove every bit of clothing they wore.

It felt like she was walking on cloud nine. A few months before, she never would have pictured her life as it was now. Happy. Full of love. Fun. Those were never things she'd considered, but now that she had them, she couldn't imagine her life any other way.

Levi was on his first shift back at the firehouse. Even though he'd only been gone for twelve hours, she'd been missing him terribly. Which was how she ended up in the community room with Ivy, Carlee, and Remi for a slumber party. None of the women worked the next day, so their Daddies had agreed to let them stay up later and have a camp out in the clubhouse.

Blankets and sheets were strewn all over the room. Chairs, couches, and tables helped keep the linens held up, creating the most epic fort Harper had ever seen. They even had string lights in it.

"Okay, girls. Here's some popcorn and a little bit of candy

for you to share," Steele said as he set down a heaping bowl but only a small handful of chocolates.

Ivy giggled and rolled her eyes. "Daddy, we need more candy than that."

He raised his eyebrows. "No, you don't. The last thing you need is candy. You four have been hyper all night as it is."

Harper smiled. They had been a bit excitable over the past few hours. But Gabriel had let them make homemade pizzas, which he was probably still regretting since they'd gone a little wild with the toppings. Then they'd gotten to sit at the table and play with clay. Of course, Remi got scolded for making inappropriate sculptures, and Carlee had gotten in trouble for throwing clay balls at her Daddy. Harper had been on her very best behavior, though.

Once the movie started, they quieted and munched on popcorn. About halfway through, Harper got up and went to the suite she was living in with Levi so she could go potty. On her way back toward the community room, Kade stopped her halfway.

"Hey, Little one. Are you having fun?"

She nodded. "Yeah. Thank you for letting Remi have a sleepover with me. I know I'm gonna have to learn to be here without Daddy."

Kade's eyebrows furrowed, and she tensed, worried she'd said something to make him angry. When he took a step toward her, she flinched. His eyes widened, and he looked as though she'd slapped him. Like he was hurt. She immediately felt awful.

"I'm sorry, Little one. I didn't mean to scare you. I was going to give you a hug."

A hug? What? She was so confused.

This time, when he reached out, she didn't move. He cupped her chin gently and smiled at her. Kade was a beautiful man when he smiled. Not that she would tell him. He probably wouldn't appreciate that sort of compliment.

"I know you don't know us yet, but none of us will ever hurt you. We'd rather cut off our own limbs before we hurt a woman. As far as you learning to be here without Doc, you don't have to. There's always at least one Little girl here to have a sleepover with, and any of the men here would be happy to come crash on the couch in your suite if you didn't want to be in there alone. What I'm trying to say is you're part of this family, and we all take care of each other. If you need anything, it doesn't matter if Doc is here or not, you can come to any of us. Okay?"

Tears formed in the corners of her eyes, and she quickly brushed them away. "Thank you. I'm sorry I flinched. It's habit."

His eyes looked sad again. "I understand, sweetheart. It'll take time. I wish I'd gotten to throw a punch or two at that fucker."

She smiled and sniffled. "Me too."

Kade chuckled and released her chin. "You know you don't have to behave here, right? You're safe to be naughty like the rest of the Little girls."

Wow. She hadn't expected that.

"Doc's made it clear to all of us that disciplining you other than time out isn't allowed. That doesn't mean we won't tell your Daddy if you do something naughty. I think I can speak for all the Daddies here. We like when our girls cause a bit of mischief. It gives us an excuse to redden their bottoms. We'd never hurt them, though. No one here will ever hurt you."

Without thinking, she threw her arms around his waist. "Thank you."

He immediately wrapped his arms around her, and she felt another small weight of the past lift off her shoulders.

Remi skipped up to them, and Harper released Kade, feeling guilty about hugging her friend's Daddy. Was it okay that she'd done that? Would Remi be mad at her?

"It's okay. You can hug my Daddy any time. Any time you

need comfort and your Daddy isn't here, you can go to him. He's the best at making Littles feel better when they're sad," Remi said as she hugged Kade's side.

Harper smiled at her friend, unable to form words, so instead, she nodded and blinked several times to keep more tears from falling.

Remi took her hand. "Come on, Harper. Let's go see if we can find more candy."

Kade growled. "Remi."

"What, Daddy?"

He eyed them and sighed, but the corners of his lips were twitching like he was fighting a smile. "You have about ten minutes to find more candy and get it eaten before I come bust you all."

It felt as though Harper's chest was about to explode with happiness. Remi wasted no time dragging her away from Kade. Harper smiled back at him, he winked at her, and something settled inside of her.

She had finally found her home.

"Give us twenty minutes, Daddy!" Remi called.

Kade laughed as the two women rushed down the hall in search of goodies.

Harper: *I miss you.*

Levi: *I miss you too, Little one. More than words can say. What are you doing right now?*

Harper: *Having another slumber party in the living room with the other Littles. I think they feel bad for me.*

Levi: *I'm sure they're loving these sleepovers as much as you are. Maybe we need to convert one of the empty suites into a slumber* party room. That way you're all close to the potty and don't get woken up by the early risers.

Harper: *It's okay, Daddy. Next time you go to work, I'll stay in our suite.*

Levi: *Okay, baby girl. Are you having fun at least?*

Harper: *Yes. Lots of fun. Bear has been letting me decorate his pancakes like cakes. It's been fun.*

Levi: *That sounds fun. Only one more sleep until I get to see you. I love you, kitten.*

Harper: *I love you too, Daddy.*

EIGHTEEN
DOC

Three days had felt like an eternity. If Doc didn't love his job so much, he'd consider finding something different so he could be home with Harper every night. But he loved helping people, and he loved his firehouse family. If only he could convince his chief to let him bring Harper with him for his shifts. Dreams could come true, right?

When he walked into the clubhouse and saw all four women sprawled out on the floor in the community room, his heart started to pound. How he got so lucky, he'd never know but he would never take it for granted.

Steele and Kade were sitting at the dining table in silence with mugs of steaming coffee, and when they saw Doc, they raised their cups to greet him. It was funny, the things all the men in the club would do to keep these Little girls happy. Sitting in silence, drinking coffee so they could sleep was one of them.

He joined his friends, and the three of them continued to sit quietly while keeping an eye on the women. As if they'd all gotten warm through the night, not a single one of them had covers on. If Doc were to guess, he'd bet money that Steele had turned up the heat because he was worried they'd get cold.

"Daddy."

He spun around and grinned as he opened his arms for his sleepy Little girl. She immediately went to him, and as soon as he had her settled on his lap, his world felt whole again. He needed her closer, though. To consume her and make up for the three days he'd been away. It felt as though he'd never get enough of her.

"Let's go to our suite. Daddy wants to snuggle you," he whispered as he rose and headed toward the hall.

She nuzzled into him and sighed.

Once they were alone, he carried her into the bathroom and set her on her feet in front of the toilet. Before she could pull down her panties, he reached under her nightie and tugged them down for her.

"Go potty, kitten."

She immediately sat then looked up at him and gave him a sleepy smile. When he heard her start to pee, he was so damn proud of her. He was pleased when he leaned down to clean her up and she didn't try to stop him. It felt like they were getting into their own groove.

After he washed his hands, he picked her up and took her into their bedroom. She still didn't have very much of her stuff there since everything in her apartment needed to be cleaned after the fire, but they were slowly moving her belongings so their suite was starting to have feminine touches that he loved.

He helped her into bed, then stripped down to his underwear and got in after her. She immediately gravitated toward him until their bodies were pressed against each other.

"I missed you so much," he said.

She let out a deep breath and tightened her arm around him. "Me too, Daddy. More than I expected. It feels like you're already so much a part of me that when you were gone, it felt like a piece of me was missing."

His heart squeezed in his chest. She'd hit the nail on the

head. It felt like he was missing his entire heart when he'd been away from her.

When she tilted her head back to look at him, he lowered his mouth to hers and captured it, kissing her deeply and thoroughly until they were both breathless.

"I heard you girls found the candy stash and went wild with the chocolate," he said with raised eyebrows.

Instead of seeming worried, she giggled. "Sorry?"

He snorted. "Are you, though?"

"Mmm, not really. It was super tasty."

"Well, Little girl, if it happens again, you know what's going to happen?"

Her eyes widened. "What?"

"Daddy's going to spank you and then clean out your bottom. When Little girls eat too much chocolate, it hurts their tummies, so the only way to fix that is to clean it out. I suggest you keep that in mind the next time."

She squirmed against him, and he nearly groaned when her hip brushed up against his already hard cock. There was something about the thought of giving his girl an enema that drove him wild. He was also looking forward to the first time he'd get to spank her cute little tush. He'd smacked her ass a few times while they'd been having sex, and she'd loved it, but there was something even better about putting a woman over his knee. And that woman being Harper was the cherry on top.

"Did you touch your pretty little pussy while I was gone?"

Her eyes widened, and she quickly shook her head. "No. You told me I wasn't allowed to."

He smiled and nodded. "That's right. You're not allowed to. Only Daddy gets to play with you unless I give you special permission."

The air around them crackled. When she spread her thighs open, he flexed his hips to grind against her core.

"Does my girl need Daddy to show her how much he missed her?"

When she bobbed her head and whimpered, he let out a growl and started kissing down her neck. As he kissed, he worked to get her nightie up and over her head. As soon as he got it off her, he captured a nipple between his teeth and bit down with enough force to make her yelp and buck her hips against his. He quickly licked away the pain before switching to the other nipple.

When she raked her fingers through his hair and pulled, he nipped at her tummy as he continued his way down to the waistband of her cotton panties. He looked up to find her watching him, her hair framing her angelic face.

"You're so beautiful, kitten. Inside and out."

She smiled softly, her eyes shining with tears. Getting compliments wasn't something she was used to.

"You're sweet," he said before he pressed a kiss right above her panties. "Kind." Another kiss. "Thoughtful." Kiss. "Strong." Kiss. "Brave." Kiss. "And best of all." Kiss. "You're mine."

Her lips rolled in as tears dripped down her cheeks. He smiled softly as he pulled her panties off, then tossed them to the floor without breaking eye contact.

"You're so wet, baby. I can see you glistening."

A small whimper escaped her as he lowered his mouth to her pussy. His cock twitched at the sharp bite of her nails digging against his scalp. She wanted his mouth on her as much as he did.

He licked her clit slowly, savoring the taste of her arousal. Her hips flexed and bucked against his face, spurring him on as he started to speed up. Moving lower, he dipped his tongue into her pussy while using his thumb to tease her clit. Her cries were like a siren's call, and he was under her spell.

When he plunged his tongue deeper, she moaned so

sweetly as she tried to raise her hips to get closer to him. He held her down, keeping her pinned to the bed.

Her cries became louder, her hands gripping and pulling on his hair, all while he continued to lick and suck on her until he felt her body tensing under him. She started screaming as her body exploded and convulsed around his tongue. He could feel the wave of her orgasm crash through her like an electrical current, and he nearly came right then and there.

Once she quieted, he pulled away and wiped his mouth with the back of his hand. His cock was leaking with his own arousal. He ripped his underwear down, letting his dick bob free between his legs. The way she stared at it made him smile. His hungry Little girl.

He raised his eyebrows. "Like what you see, baby?"

"Yes. I want to taste it," she said so quietly he almost didn't hear.

He was so fucking proud that she was asking for what she wanted. As he moved toward her, his eyes locked with hers. When he was standing near her, she glanced down at his length and swallowed. With a trembling hand, she reached out and wrapped her tiny fingers around him. Suddenly, Doc wasn't sure if he was going to be able to let her taste him for much more than a second or two because he was riding the edge of his own ecstasy. Plus, he wanted to be inside her when he came.

He groaned softly as she began to stroke him, her delicate grip making him nearly come apart. She looked up at him as hungry as he was. Slowly, she lowered her head, her pink tongue darting out to wet her lips before she took him into her mouth.

As she started to suck, he clenched his fists and tried to think about anything to keep from exploding in her mouth. She started to bob her head, taking him a little deeper each time, her cheeks hollowing out as she sucked.

Not wanting to overwhelm her, he gently placed his hand

on her head but didn't apply pressure. To his surprise, she reached back and pressed her hand on top of his. He furrowed his eyebrows.

"You want me to be rough, baby? Is that what you're asking for?"

She nodded, her blue eyes staring up at him, wide and innocent. Fuck. He was going to come apart before he got to fuck her.

He stroked her cheek and couldn't resist the temptation she was offering. He squeezed a fistful of hair and thrust into her mouth. She gasped, a soft moan escaping her when he pulled back to give her air.

"Like that, baby? You want Daddy to be rough with you like that?"

"Uh huh," she mumbled around him.

"If you need me to stop, tap my thigh two times. Understand?"

She gave a slight nod before she closed her eyes and sucked him harder. Letting out a growl, he started to fuck her mouth. Slow but firm, holding her head in place so she couldn't move. It was taking every ounce of restraint not to come as he watched her sucking him off like it was her favorite pastime.

"Fuck, baby. Fuck!" he grunted. "I'm not going to last. We need to stop before I come down your tight little throat."

The only response he got was her wrapping her arm around him and clawing at his ass to keep him from pulling away.

"Is that what you want, Little girl? You want me to come down your throat?"

"Mmmm."

Jesus Christ. This woman was going to kill him. But damn, he was going to die a very happy man.

"You're going to swallow every drop," he told her.

Her blue eyes flashed up to his, and he couldn't control himself any longer. He tightened his grip and fucked her mouth harder and faster. It didn't take long before the first bit of semen shot down her throat.

"Fuck!" he shouted as he poured himself into her.

When his climax finally subsided, he stepped back and took her face in his hands. Without caring that he'd come in her mouth, he kissed her deeply. She whimpered and sighed as he fell into bed with her, keeping their lips locked the entire time.

They were breathless when he pulled back to stare at her. A soft smile tugged at the corners of her lips.

"That was," he said breathlessly, "fucking amazing."

She giggled and crawled over him so her face was resting against his chest. "It was the hottest experience I've ever had."

He wrapped his arms around her and squeezed. "And we're just getting started, baby girl."

NINETEEN
HARPER

Two weeks later...

"Are you sure this is a good idea?" Harper asked as she glanced toward the community room where several of the guys were watching a movie.

"They wouldn't leave it here if they didn't want us to find it," Carlee said.

Harper fidgeted with the hem of her dress and sighed. "Daddy said if I snuck candy again, he was going to give me an enema."

Carlee's eyes widened, but she was smiling. "Has he given you one yet?"

"No. He takes my temperature in my bottom every day, though."

Remi nodded. "Yeah. That doesn't surprise me. He is a medic after all."

"Ah ha!" Ivy whisper shouted as she pulled out a big bowl of chocolate.

"Hurry, grab a handful and put it in your pockets before someone comes in here," Remi said as she reached for the candy.

All four women stuffed their pockets full before they quickly returned the bowl to its rightful spot.

"Let's go in the playroom. We can pretend we're having Book Club," Carlee said as she started off in that direction.

Harper glanced toward her Daddy, who was talking to Bear and not paying attention to what they were up to. Usually, his eyes were on her all the time, so maybe this was a sign that she wouldn't get caught.

It wasn't lost on her that while she knew she'd get into trouble if she got caught, it didn't scare her. She was safe with Levi. He loved her. The real kind of love she'd always dreamed of.

They made it into the playroom and settled on the floor in a circle. Carlee reached behind her, grabbed four books from the shelf, and then passed them around. Harper giggled when she looked down at the one she ended up with. *Disciplining His Little*. That was hitting a bit close to home considering she had a pocket full of candy she wasn't supposed to have.

Storm appeared in the doorway of the playroom, a deep scowl on his face. The first time Harper had met him, she'd been terrified of the man, but he wasn't as scary as he appeared. Although he was a big grumpy pants. Not that she would tell him. Nope. She didn't have a death wish.

"Which one of you brats put your red sock in with my whites?" he demanded as he held up a pink shirt.

Harper's eyes widened. When she glanced around at the other women, they were grinning, completely unfazed by him.

"Why would you think it was us? Maybe you don't know how to separate your laundry correctly," Remi said.

His nostrils flared. "Remi, don't think I won't throw you over my shoulder and take you directly to your Daddy to have your ass spanked."

"Oooh, you said a bad word!" Carlee snapped. "You have to put money in the swear jar now."

Harper covered her mouth to hide the laughter threatening to break free as he furrowed his eyebrows in confusion.

"What the fuck are you talking about? We don't have a swear jar."

Ivy nodded and pointed to one of the higher shelves that held a glass jar with a *Swear Jar* sign taped to it. "Ya, huh. We aren't allowed to cuss so you guys can't either. It's five dollars every time you swear. Ten when you say the f-word. So cough it up. Fifteen bucks."

Storm stared down at them, his dark eyes narrowed as he pulled out his wallet. "You know what. Here's a fifty to get me by for a day or two. Now, who put the goddamn red sock in with my clothes?"

"Not sure what you're talking about Uncle Storm. Pink is definitely your color, though," Carlee replied.

He sighed and moved his gaze to Harper, then raised an eyebrow. "Do you know who did it?"

She lowered her gaze, and then glanced at her friends, who were struggling to keep from laughing.

After taking a deep breath, she turned toward him and smiled. "Maybe you need glasses? I heard when you get old you can't identify colors as well."

Storm's eyes widened, clearly surprised by her sassy answer. He ran a hand over his dark hair and huffed. "When did you become a brat? I thought you were the good one of the group. I'm not old."

Harper scrunched her face. "But you have gray hairs."

The three other women burst out laughing as he stomped off, muttering under his breath about brats needing their asses spanked. Harper started giggling right along with them.

"That was fun," Ivy said as she wiped tears from her eyes.

"Did you guys really put a red sock in with his whites?" Harper asked.

Remi grinned. "Actually, no. Talon did. He was getting Storm back for something. But it was fun to mess with him."

When they finally got themselves under control, they got comfy on the floor and chatted while sneaking piece after piece of chocolate, shoving the wrappers under one of the chairs.

"We do need to figure out what book to read next for Book Club," Remi said.

Ivy bobbed her head. "We could do the next in that series. It's called *Maddie's Daddy Crush*."

"Works for me. We might have to read through the author's entire catalog. I saw she has a series called *Daddies of the Shadows*, and it's about a bunch of tattooed, overprotective, vigilante Daddies who are super badass, but also super sweet with their Littles," Carlee added.

Harper nodded and shoved another piece of chocolate in her mouth at the same time as the other women before they shoved the wrappers under the chair.

"Well, well, well," Levi interrupted, causing them all to squeal in surprise.

Harper spun around to find her Daddy standing in the doorway along with Steele, Atlas, and Kade, and they didn't look pleased.

"Oh! You scared us," Carlee said with her hand over her heart.

Atlas raised an eyebrow. "Usually, you wouldn't be so jumpy unless you were doing something wrong. So, what were you doing wrong?"

Remi rolled her eyes. "God, my brother is so annoying. We aren't doing anything wrong. Paranoid much?"

"Remi," Kade growled in a low tone.

Levi stared down at Harper, his eyes sparkling with promise. A promise she wasn't so sure she was ready for.

She glanced at the men's legs. Could she make a run for it and squeeze between them?

"Don't even think about running, kitten," Levi warned.

A shiver ran through her. Crap. She was in for it.

"How much candy have you eaten?" Steele asked.

Ivy shook her head. "None, Daddy. We're having Book Club."

Levi raised an eyebrow as he stared down at Harper. "Little girl?"

"We're having Book Club, Daddy," she repeated.

He crossed his arms over his chest. "Kitten, you're riding a fine line, and once you cross it, you're going to be very sorry."

Shoot. Crap.

Either way, she was going to be in trouble. Her Daddy had warned her. Might as well keep up the charade.

"I think this room needs a little updating," Atlas said.

Steele nodded. "I agree. What are you thinking? Rearrange the furniture a bit?"

Harper's eyes bugged out as she glanced at the other women. They all looked as worried as she felt.

"Yeah. A little sprucing up will make this place real nice. Let's move this chair to that corner. It will really open it up in here," Levi replied without moving his gaze from hers.

It only took seconds before Steele and Kade had the chair lifted and moved, exposing their pile of empty chocolate wrappers.

"Harper Ann," Levi growled.

Uh oh. Using her middle name was never a good sign. She twisted her hands together and gave him the biggest, most innocent smile she could.

"Well, you see, Daddy. We were hungry, and we read that chocolate actually comes from plants, which means it's healthy. You guys were super busy, and it would have been rude to interrupt you to ask for food, so we were being polite," she rambled.

"Uh huh," Ivy added.

"Maybe we should count the wrappers and for each one, the girls get five spanks," Kade said.

Harper's mouth dropped open. That was gonna be...like... a lot of spankings.

Levi smiled down at her. "I don't know. I mean, with all that chocolate, their tummies are going to be hurting badly unless we do something about it. I'm thinking a sound spanking and then enemas for each of them."

"I think that's a great idea. Then they can all take a nap afterward," Atlas said.

"On your feet," Steele commanded in a tone that left absolutely no room for argument.

All at once, the women stood. Harper noticed Remi slide her hands back to cover her bottom as she faced her Daddy.

"Let's go, Little one," Levi said as he held out his hand to her.

She eyed it for a second before she slid her palm into his and let him lead her to her doom. Okay, doom was a little dramatic, but then again, she *was* a Little girl so it felt dramatic.

As he led her to their suite, he stayed silent. When he closed the door behind them, she jumped at the sound.

"Calm down, baby. Look at me," he said in a calm voice.

Slowly, she raised her gaze to meet his. Instead of seeing anger or disappointment, all she saw was love.

"Who am I?" he asked.

Her response was immediate. "Daddy."

He nodded and smiled. "That's right. I'm Daddy, and my job is to take care of you. Never to hurt or harm you. Never to abuse you or your trust. Right?"

His words soothed her, and she instantly relaxed. "Yes, Daddy."

"No matter what, even during discipline, you're allowed to say your safeword. That means if you get scared enough that you want it to stop, you can say red, and everything stops immediately. If you get anxious or it's too much, all you have to say is red. I'll never be angry with you, and you'll never be in trouble if you use that word unless you use it to manipulate me in some way."

She nodded. "I wouldn't do that."

When he reached out and cupped her chin, she automatically nuzzled into his palm.

"I don't think you ever would, but I wanted to make it clear. Now, what did I tell you would happen if I caught you sneaking candy?"

Her cheeks heated. Was he going to make her say it out loud?

"I'd be in trouble," she answered.

He smiled and squeezed her chin. "Nice try. What *specifically* did I tell you would happen?"

Shoot.

"You would give me an enema and a spanking," she answered, her voice wobbling.

"That's correct. Do either of those punishments make you feel the need to use your safeword right now?"

She thought about it for a few seconds. Being spanked intrigued her. She'd always fantasized about being taken across a man's knees. The enema, though. She was part curious and part horrified. Her Daddy, the man who was supposed to find her sexy, was going to put something in her bottom to clean her out. How embarrassing. But at the same time, she felt herself growing warm all over at the idea of her Daddy doing something so incredibly intimate to her.

"No, Daddy. I don't want to use it."

His eyes sparkled with something she wasn't used to seeing from a man. He was proud of her. And that meant more than she could ever put into words. She couldn't remember the last time someone had been proud of *her*.

After he led her into their bedroom, she started fidgeting with the hem of her shirt. Even though she knew her Daddy wouldn't harm her, there was still a part of her that was scared. For some reason, the fear seemed to make it even more exciting.

He moved over to the edge of the bed, sat, then patted his thighs. "Come here, kitten."

Taking a deep breath, she went to him and stood between his legs. He set his hands on her hips. Having him touching her helped to soothe her nerves.

"I want you to know I'm not mad, upset, disappointed, or anything like that. You broke a rule, but the only time I will truly be upset is if you break a health or safety rule. Eating a bunch of chocolates is a small, naughty thing that Little girls do sometimes."

"So then maybe you don't have to punish me?" she asked hopefully.

He chuckled and shook his head. "Nice try, Little one. When I give you a rule, whether it's just a Daddy rule or a safety rule, I expect it to be obeyed, and if it's not, you will have consequences."

She let out a long sigh and nodded.

"Any last words?"

"Um, the chocolate was really yummy."

When he burst out laughing, she started giggling.

He gave her hips a slight squeeze. "You, my Little girl, are the most precious thing in my world. Don't ever stop being yourself, okay?"

"You make me feel safe to be myself," she answered.

They stared at each other for a long moment, and she could see the emotions running through him.

"I love you, kitten."

"I love you, too, Daddy."

"Good, because this is where I bare your bottom and put you over my knee for a good, long spanking."

Before she could respond, he lifted her shirt and pushed her pants and panties down to her thighs. She let out a soft whimper when he pulled her over his lap. Her feet dangled in the air, and she couldn't reach the floor with her hands, so instead she wrapped her arms around his calf for leverage.

"How are you doing, baby?"

"Good."

He gently patted her bottom. She jolted in surprise. Sheesh. Nervous, much?

"I'm glad to hear it. I'll ask again later and see if I get the same answer," he said, his voice full of humor.

Just as she was getting ready to look back and glare at him, his hand landed on her bottom with a loud *smack*.

"Oh!" she cried out.

He ignored her and smacked the other cheek just as hard. The sting of his palm started spreading through her. She didn't have time to think about it because he was steadily spanking her with so much force she began kicking her feet.

"Ow! Daddy!"

"The next time Daddy says no sneaking chocolate, I hope this serves as a reminder that when I give you a rule, I mean it. Naughty Little girls who misbehave get their bottoms reddened," he scolded as he continued to spank her.

She kicked and squirmed, but the hold he had on her was so tight she didn't stand a chance.

"Owwie!"

It only took a few minutes before tears filled her eyes and spilled down her cheeks. When she let out a sob, he stopped spanking her and flipped her up onto his lap, where she immediately snuggled into his chest.

"Shh, I've got you. You did so well, baby girl."

She wasn't so sure considering she'd been squirming and fighting it the entire time, but if he said so, he must have meant it.

He held her for several minutes, rocking her back and forth until her tears dried and her sniffling stopped. When he leaned back and kissed the tip of her nose, she nearly exploded with love for him. Then, he said the words she'd been dreading.

"Time for your enema, Little one. Let's go into the bathroom."

Instead of putting her down, he carried her, then set her on her feet. He knelt in front of her and pulled her leggings and panties the rest of the way down.

"Hold my shoulders and step out."

She obeyed, loving the strong feel of him under her fingers. Her doom might be coming, but he would be with her every step of the way, and for some reason, that made her feel a lot better.

"Okay, I want you to bend over and rest your arms on the edge of the tub. Then push out your bottom."

If her cheeks could burst into flames, she was pretty sure they would. Thankfully that wasn't a real thing. Would he see the arousal she could feel between her legs?

Slowly, she turned and faced the tub, then dropped to her knees and got into the position he'd described. A few seconds later, she heard the water in the sink running. When she looked back to see what he was doing, her eyes widened. There was tubing and a thick butt-plug-looking thing on the counter. He was filling a red rubber bag full of water.

"Eyes forward, kitten," he said without glancing at her.

She whipped her head forward, not wanting to get into any more trouble. Her bottom was still on fire, and she was pretty sure it was bright red too.

Her entire body trembled as she waited for him. When the water stopped and she heard him moving toward her, she sucked in a breath.

"Here's how this is going to go. Daddy is going to put this," he said, holding the black plug-looking thing out for her to see, "into your bottom and inflate it slightly so it opens up the walls of your insides. Then, I'm going to slowly let this bag of saline solution go into your bottom. After that, you're going to hold it in for up to ten minutes unless you can't go that long, and I'll put you on the toilet to release it. Any questions?"

Holy heck. Was it too late to run? That was her question. She didn't think it would be a wise one to ask, though, so instead, she shook her head. "No, Daddy," she squeaked.

"Good. It's going to be cold while I spread lube on your bottom hole," he said right before she felt a drip of liquid hit her back there.

When he started spreading it around, she bit her lip to keep herself from moaning. Why did that feel so good? She shouldn't be getting turned on from all of this. She was supposed to be getting punished.

As he pressed the tip of the black plug to her hole, she whimpered.

"Breathe, baby. Deep breath in, and then let it out," he crooned as he rubbed one of her bottom cheeks.

She obeyed, and when she let out her breath, he pressed the plug in until it settled in place. It felt foreign and uncomfortable, but it didn't hurt. When the device started to expand inside of her, she couldn't stop the quiet moan that escaped her lips.

"Maybe next time you don't want to get caught being naughty, you girls shouldn't write your plans in that secret journal."

Her mouth fell open as she turned to look at him.

He was so smug as he winked at her. "Daddy knows everything."

She let out a sigh. "Do all the Daddies know?"

"Probably." He shrugged. "We keep a pretty close eye on all of you around here."

Well, crap.

"Here comes the liquid."

Any thoughts of the journal disappeared as the warm solution started to fill her.

"You're doing so good, kitten. Daddy's proud of you," he praised.

She whimpered and sniffled in response as her insides got fuller and fuller until he announced all the liquid was inside her.

"Can I have Whiskers, Daddy?" she asked.

"You may. I'll get her after I wash my hands."

A moment later, Daddy held her stuffie in front of her, then pressed a kiss to the top of her head. She felt so incredibly full, almost like the liquid was sloshing inside of her.

"Can I go potty yet?" she whimpered.

"Not yet. Ten minutes or until you can't hold it any longer."

She moaned. She wanted to go potty and get this over with, but she knew she could still hold it for a bit longer.

"How do you feel, baby?"

"Full."

He chuckled. "Yeah. But just think, now your tummy won't hurt later from all that chocolate you consumed."

She wasn't so sure about that.

A cramp hit her out of nowhere, and the sudden urge to go to the bathroom was so strong that she started to panic. She wasn't going to make it to the toilet.

"Daddy," she cried out. "I *really* need to go. *Please.*"

"Okay, baby. Let me help you. I'm going to stand you in front of the toilet and pull out the plug. As soon as I do, you can sit down."

Her cheeks were flaming, but she was panicking so much about making it to the toilet that she couldn't bother to be embarrassed by all of this.

He helped her up and led her to the toilet, then gently pulled the plug free. As soon as he straightened, she sat.

"Get out!" she cried, trying desperately to hold it in until he was gone.

"Sorry, baby. Part of the punishment is you releasing it with me here. It's nothing I haven't seen before."

Her mouth fell open in disbelief that he would actually force her to do this in front of him, but another cramp hit, and she couldn't hold it for another second. She covered her face with her hands and let out a whimper as she lost her control and emptied herself into the toilet. With her Daddy standing right in front of her.

EPILOGUE

A *week later...*

"Keep them closed."

Harper squeezed her eyes shut and gripped his hand.

"They are closed. Where are we going?"

"You'll see. Take another step."

He smiled as she took a slow, unsure step forward.

"Daddy, what's going on?" Ivy asked as Steele led his Little girl in the same direction Doc was leading his.

Kade and Remi were next, Kade keeping his hands on her shoulders to get her to move in the direction he wanted her to go.

"Why am I blindfolded?" Carlee whined as Atlas carried her on his hip.

"Why is Carlee here?" Ivy asked.

"I'm here, too," Harper said.

"Me too," Remi added.

The men grinned at each other. Storm, Gabriel, Talon, King,

Bear, and Faust all joined them, looking mighty proud of themselves for the help they put in.

"Ready?" Doc asked.

"Yes," all four women answered at the same time.

The men chuckled.

"Okay, you can look," Steele announced.

Harper opened her eyes and gasped as she took it all in.

"What is this?" Ivy asked.

"This," Doc said, "is your new slumber room. For when you want to have a sleepover. The shelves are stocked full of movies, and there are toy baskets full of toys and activities."

Remi started walking around. "This looks like one of the suites."

"That's because it is one of the suites. We got rid of the living room furniture, removed the wall that separated the bedroom to make it one big room, and brought in bunk beds so you can all sleep on a mattress instead of the floor," Kade told her.

Harper smiled up at Doc with tears in her eyes. "You did this for me?"

He grinned at her and pulled her close. "Well, it was my idea, but all the guys helped. You may not be able to have a slumber party every night I'm at work, but when you're able to, I wanted you to have a magical space to do it rather than the cold floor in the community room."

"It's so beautiful. I can't believe you hung twinkle lights above each bed," she whispered in awe as she stared at the bunks.

"I know my girl doesn't like the dark when she sleeps," he replied.

Warmth filled him as Harper, Remi, Ivy, and Carlee explored the room, pulling out puzzles and movies and toys. He hated leaving his baby girl when he had to go to work, but he felt better knowing she had this space to spend time with her friends while sleeping comfortably at the same time.

A moment later, she ran toward him and jumped into his arms, wrapping her legs around his waist. "Thank you, Daddy. I love you so much."

He twirled her in his arms and grinned. "I love you, too. I'm going to spend the rest of my life doing whatever I can to keep that beautiful smile on your face."

"Promise?"

"Promise. Forever and always. You're mine."

Ready for Gabriel's book?

"Carlee?" Eden could barely get her friend's name out between sobs as she held her cell phone close to her ear.

"Eden? What's wrong? Where are you?" Carlee asked.

Eden stopped walking and looked around, sniffling. "I need help," she admitted reluctantly. "I'm scared." She couldn't stop shaking.

There was a shuffling sound, and then Carlee's boyfriend was on the phone. "Eden, honey, where are you?" Atlas asked.

Tears streamed down her cheeks. "About a block from the diner, I think." A sob escaped. "I ran out. I think I went left. I wasn't thinking."

"Okay, honey, I'm sending someone to help you. His name is Gabriel Marcos. Stay right where you are and keep talking to me," he ordered.

Eden had met Atlas several times. She knew he was a good guy and treated Carlee like spun gold. She also knew he was a member of the Shadowridge Guardians MC.

Before Carlee had started dating Atlas, Eden had always been a bit nervous when members of the Shadowridge

Guardians came into the diner. She'd since realized they were some of the best guys on the planet.

"Eden?" Atlas prodded. "Are you with me, honey?"

"Y-yes, Sir."

"Good girl. Keep talking to me."

"Is G-Gabriel one of your, uh, brothers?" *Is that what they call each other?*

"He sure is, honey. He's a super good guy. I promise."

"O-okay." She sniffled again as she hugged herself. She was still wearing her apron. She hadn't even stopped to grab her purse before she'd run out of the diner.

"I can hear the motorcycle engine through the phone, honey. He's almost there."

Eden realized he was right. She was glad he was still talking to her. The approaching motorcycle might have scared her otherwise. Sure enough, it was coming into view from her left.

"H-he's here," she muttered as the motorcycle pulled to a stop.

"Okay, honey. Let Gabriel help you."

The man who parked alongside her kicked out the stand, rose from the bike, and pulled his helmet off in seconds. He rushed over to her. "Eden?"

She wanted to stop crying, but she couldn't. More tears fell. She was trembling so badly she almost dropped her phone.

The tall man gently took the cell from her and spoke into it. "I've got her, Atlas." He ended the call and pocketed the phone before squatting in front of her. "You're safe, Eden. Can you tell me what happened?"

Suddenly, she felt stupid. Maybe she'd overreacted. She started crying harder now. "I-I d-didn't know w-what to d-do. I'm sorry." She swiped at the tears, trying to banish them, but more kept coming.

"You did the right thing, Little one. You called for help."

"I'm s-sorry to be a b-bother."

"No reason to be sorry." He rose to his full height, turned around, and opened the saddlebag on his bike. A moment later, he held out a cute, fluffy, brown teddy bear. "How about you hold this little fellow for me? I bet he'll make you feel better."

She took him and pulled him against her chest. He was adorable. "W-whose b-bear is this?"

"Yours, Little one. I bet he's super happy to finally get out of my bag and into the hands of a Little girl."

"I'm n-not l-little. I'm twenty-six, Sir." She suspected that when he called her little he wasn't referring to size or age. After all, she was aware that Carlee's relationship with Atlas was a special kind of arrangement in which she called Atlas her Daddy, and he took care of her like a Little girl.

Pre-Order Gabriel by Becca Jameson now!

ALSO BY KATE OLIVER

West Coast Daddies Series

Ally's Christmas Daddy

Haylee's Hero Daddy

Maddie's Daddy Crush

Safe With Daddy

Trusting Her Daddy

Ruby's Forever Daddies

Daddies of the Shadows Series

Knox

Ash

Beau

Wolf

Leo

Maddox

Colt

Hawk

Angel

Tate

Rawhide Ranch

A Little Fourth of July Fiasco

Shadowridge Guardians

(A multi-author series)

Kade

Doc

Syndicate Kings

Corrupting Cali: Declan's Story

Saving Scarlet: Killian's Story

Controlling Chloe: Bash's Story

Possessing Paisley: Kieran's Story

Daddies of Pine Hollow

Jaxon

Dane

Nash

KEEP UP WITH KATE!

Sign up for my newsletter get teasers, cover reveals, updates, and extra content!

SCAN ME TO SIGN UP NOW!

PLEASE LEAVE A REVIEW!

It would mean so much to me if you would take a brief moment to leave a rating and/or a review on this book. It helps other readers find me. Thank you for your support!

-Kate

Printed in Great Britain
by Amazon